"Hello," I called. "Anyone there?"

In answer, I heard a metallic clatter, as though someone were gathering up tools, and then the footsteps of someone running.

"Who's there?" I called. But the footsteps were already hurriedly mounting the stairs at the far end of the hall. I kept walking. I passed another doorway, probably the furnace room. I raised my flashlight and saw the stone stairs along the far wall. Lowering the beam, I spotted something on the floor near the interior wall that supported the stairs. It looked like one of the rectangular stones that formed the walls down here. I wondered if it had become loose from thirty years underwater.

But it didn't appear that way. There were chunks of mortar on the ground around the stone, as though someone had just dug it out. When I had nearly reached it, my light caught something gold on the floor. I picked it up and pocketed it. Then I sat on my heels and pointed the flashlight into the opening under the stairs.

I drew in my breath and said, "Oh, no," and at the same moment I crossed myself.

Inside the exposed opening, dirty and fleshless, was all that remained of a body that had been underwater for three decades.

Also by Lee Harris
Published by Fawcett Books:

THE GOOD FRIDAY MURDER
THE YOM KIPPUR MURDER

THE CHRISTENING DAY MURDER

Lee Harris

FAWCETT GOLD MEDAL • NEW YORK

A Fawcett Gold Medal Book
Published by Ballantine Books
Copyright © 1993 by Lee Harris

All rights reserved under International and Pan-American Copyright Conventions. Published in the United States of America by Ballantine Books, a division of Random House, Inc., New York, and simultaneously in Canada by Random House of Canada Limited, Toronto.

Library of Congress Catalog Card Number: 93-90204

ISBN: 0-449-14871-8

Manufactured in the United States of America

First Edition: October 1993

For Paige
With affection and thanks

The author wishes to thank
Ana M. Soler and James L. V. Wegman
for their invaluable help.

We are what suns and winds and waters make us

Regeneration
WALTER SAVAGE LANDOR
1775–1864

1

It began with a phone call out of the blue, a voice I hadn't heard for many months. The phone rang as I was clearing up my dinner dishes. I grabbed a towel, rubbing my fingers on it as I went.

"Kix?" a somewhat breathless voice said in my ear.

I smiled at the name. People who call me Kix knew me when I was a kid or else were fellow nuns at St. Stephen's. Everyone else calls me Chris. The breathlessness had given her away. "Maddie? Is that you?"

"It is and I've done it. I'm a mother!" She sounded as though she'd just won an Olympic gold. "It's wonderful," my friend said. "He's big and beautiful and healthy and his name is Richard—we're calling him Richie. This is better than when we switched the midterms in Miss Ames's English class and she nearly suspended me."

"Oh, Maddie, congratulations. That's wonderful." I was laughing now, seeing the skinny, giggly girl she used to be, with lots of hair and lots of trouble up her sleeve.

"Look, I know I haven't called for months, but I've really dedicated myself to getting through this pregnancy."

As she spoke, I recalled her problems of years past, the difficulty conceiving, then later miscarrying. There had been a letter that had frightened me because of its downbeat tone and almost garbled handwriting.

"It's OK," I said. "I've been remiss myself."

"I see you got away," my very upbeat friend said. "You're out now, aren't you?"

1

"Yes. I left the order last June."

"They told me. I knew it was in the works, but I didn't know it had happened. Are you living with your aunt?"

"She died, Maddie. I'm living in the house she left me."

"Oh. Gee, I'm sorry. It must have been tough for you. Kix," she said, and her voice picked up again, "I'm calling to invite you to the christening."

"I'd love to come," I said, delighted at the invitation. "Let me get a pencil."

"We're not having it in the local church, Kix. We're doing it in upstate New York, about a hundred fifty miles or so from you. If you don't have a car, we can—"

"I have one and I'd love to make the trip. What's the name of the town?"

"Studsburg. I'll send you directions. It's a little spooky. Do you mind spooky things?"

"Not if you're there to hold my hand." Listening to the excited voice had raised my own blood pressure a notch and given me a giddy edge. "Does your mother live there now?"

"Nobody lives there. Nobody's lived there for thirty years. Studsburg doesn't really exist anymore." I must have been quiet for too long, because she said, "Are you still with me?"

"I'm here, but I think I lost you."

"I'm thirty, right?"

"Right."

"We're both thirty. I was born in Studsburg, and I was the last baby christened in St. Mary Immaculate Church there. The day after my christening, Studsburg was emptied and the Army Corps of Engineers flooded it for a reservoir."

"You mean the whole town is underwater?" I was starting to wonder if Maddie had all her marbles.

"It was for thirty years, but then the drought came."

"I know. I've been saving dishwater to water my plants."

"Well, it's much worse in upstate New York. It's so bad, the town came back."

I felt a chill. "You mean the whole reservoir dried up?"

"Just as if someone had pulled the plug in a bathtub. You can walk in it without getting your feet wet."

"That's amazing," I said. "But what could be left after so long a time underwater?"

"I haven't seen it yet myself," Maddie said, "but from what I hear from my cousins and Grandmother Stifler, there are a lot of foundations of houses, parts of some streets, a couple of bridges, and one perfectly beautiful St. Mary Immaculate Church."

The chill deepened. "That's remarkable."

"Minus its windows, of course. Mom said they were taken out before the flooding because they were very valuable. And of course, the pews were removed. My mother still has one in her living room. But the whole stone exterior is pretty much intact. We heard the steeple was the first thing that showed when the water level went down. Now there isn't any more than a few puddles, and tourists pour in every weekend to take pictures."

"Absolutely amazing," I said for at least the second time. "And you were the last baby to be baptized there."

"And Richie will be the next. My mother truly believes it's a miracle."

"Maddie, you couldn't keep me away from that christening."

"I'm glad to hear it. And Kix . . ." She paused. "You sound really terrific. Loose, you know?"

I smiled. "I'm doing fine."

"I know you thought a lot about leaving the convent, but did you go because . . . I mean, is there someone in your life?"

"I didn't leave for a man," I said, not answering the second part of her question. "It was what I told you, a matter of conscience. I thought about it for a couple of years."

"What are you doing with yourself?"

"A little teaching, a little volunteer work, a little gardening. I'm really enjoying myself."

"We'll have to talk. I'll mail you the directions to Studsburg and I'll put you up with one of my cousins who lives nearby.''

"Don't do that, Maddie. I'd prefer a motel room. I'll make it a vacation weekend. I'm really looking forward to it."

"Great. Good talking to you."

I felt wonderfully elated after hanging up. I could remember skinny little Maddie Stifler as though we were still in Miss Ames's English class. Maddie had been fun and trouble in equal parts, and I guess something in me envied her casual, disruptive behavior and easy style of friendship. What had drawn us to each other, I had no idea. I knew her during the unhappiest years of my life, through my mother's illness and death, and then the year I lived with my aunt and uncle and their retarded son, Gene, my cousin, who now lived in a group home not far from Oakwood. There were times when Maddie's behavior went beyond shocking me, but at the worst of times, she could always make me giggle. I had never met anyone who had threatened so often and so sincerely to run away from home, to get away from *that woman* who was her mother. All I had wanted was for my own mother to survive her illness, to live another day, to be with me when I needed her.

But Maddie had grown up as we all had, and in doing so she had calmed down, married Frank Clark, suffered her own sadness and disruption, and reconciled happily with her mother. And in two weeks we would celebrate the happiest of the seven sacraments, the baptism of her son.

When I had finished the dishes, I went upstairs to the room I still thought of as my aunt's sewing room. Aunt Margaret had been a notorious pack rat, and although I had lived in the house I inherited from her for many months, I had been reluctant to throw out all the fruits of her labor. In a box marked MAPS, I found at least twenty, some of them dating back to early in her marriage.

She and Uncle Will had obviously saved every map from every trip they ever took. Because traveling with Gene was difficult, most of their trips had been by car, and there were road maps dating back to the fifties. Most of them were the kind you used to get free from gas stations, and sure enough, there was one for New York State from more than thirty years ago.

I looked up Studsburg in the alphabetical listing of cities and towns, and traced over and up to the square where the letter along the side and the number along the bottom met. The little dot was south and west of Ithaca and north and west of Binghamton, Elmira, and Corning. It was on a little gray line that was listed as "other roads" on the legend. I suspected it hadn't improved much in thirty years, especially with the demise of Studsburg.

Not far to the south was the Pennsylvania border, and a few towns with familiar names roughly encircled Studsburg. Painted Post, Olean, and Hornell were some of them. Watkins Glen wasn't all that far away to the northeast; I might make a stopover on my way home.

What I was really thinking about was the possibility of having company. I was pretty sure Maddie wouldn't mind, and the thought of spending a weekend, even a single night, in a hotel with Jack was raising more than my blood pressure.

Jack Brooks is a sergeant with the New York City Police Department. We met when I was a few weeks out of St. Stephen's and looking into a forty-year-old murder I had gotten hooked into investigating. The last thing I wanted at that point in my life was a relationship with a man. I had just made the most important decision of my life, leaving the convent where I had spent half of that life, and I wanted time to become part of my new community before thinking about emotional attachments. Happily, I turned out not to be very good at planning, and our friendship blossomed into a love affair. Having lived without sex for thirty years, I am still somewhat amazed that I can be reduced to desperation if we don't see each other for more than a few days. But we had never spent a night anywhere but in my house or his apartment, and I had fantasies about making love in a hotel.

I put the map back in the box and went downstairs to read

the paper and watch something on TV. It was one of Jack's nights at law school, so I couldn't call till after ten, when he would get home so tired that it was often hard for him to make conversation.

I waited till the top news had been reported and then dialed his number. He answered on the second ring—he lives in a tiny apartment.

"It's me," I said. "You sound beat."

"I'm fine. How are you?"

"Got an invitation I want to share with you. A weekend in the middle of New York State and a christening on Sunday morning."

"The weekend sounds great. When is it?"

"Two weeks from Sunday."

I heard a page turn in the little book he keeps in his pocket. Then I heard the hiss of an obscenity. "I've got a big test the week after, Chris. I already put in for a day off so I can study. I don't see how I can do it." He sounded down, and I felt the sting of my own disappointment.

"Don't worry it," I said. "There'll be lots of other times."

"Will you mind going without me?"

"Sure I'll mind. But I'll go anyway, and miss you."

"You got anything on for tomorrow night?"

"Nothing."

"No town meetings or faculty get-togethers or plea bargains with your *pro bono* friend?"

I laughed. "My calendar is clear."

"Why don't you come on in and we'll have dinner and stay warm together?"

"I'll be there."

"It feels like weeks since I saw you."

It was four days. "Me, too."

"I'll be home by six-thirty."

"I'll be waiting."

Among the things I do in my life are teaching, which I've done for years, and some work for a lawyer named Arnold

Gold, who has become a friend of mine. Arnold is the quint-
essential champion of the underdog and one of the best lawyers around. He got me started on some volunteer work some
time ago and then began to worry about how I was supporting myself. I told him I had little to worry about. The house
I live in is paid for. My aunt left me some money, which
yields interest, and when I left St. Stephen's, the remainder
of my dowry was returned to me, minus expenses like my
car. Added to my inheritance, it seemed pretty substantial to
me, although I guess to most people it might not. But Arnold
was worried about my future. Did I have medical insurance?
How about social security? What if I was hit with a cata-
strophic illness? When I had no satisfactory answers for his
questions, he hired me to do some part-time work, get in on
his profit-sharing plan, pay my social security, and get myself
insured.

Mostly I take things home with me and type them up, but
I've also done some proofreading and editing, and on occasion even running to the post office or delivering something
that should have been done yesterday. On the day after the
call from Maddie, I had a stack of work that I intended to
return to Arnold's office. Usually I take the train in from my
little town of Oakwood on the north shore of the Long Island
Sound, but since I was going to see Jack, I drove in, parked
near his apartment in Brooklyn Heights, and took the subway
back to Manhattan. Arnold was in court, but there was work
for me, and I spent a few hours at the computer before taking
the subway back to Brooklyn.

Jack's apartment is two rooms, with a tiny kitchen on one
wall of the living room. It has everything in miniature that
the ideal kitchen would have, including a microwave oven
and a dishwasher. The place is always spotlessly clean, although I'm sure he cooks there and I know he lives there.
When I left St. Stephen's, I relaxed a little in a lot of ways.
If papers pile up or clothes go unironed, I don't worry much
about it.

I took a quick shower and washed off the grime of New

York. Then I put on jeans and a sweatshirt. If we were going out for dinner, I could change. But it felt good to relax in something casual, and while I waited, I made a cup of tea and read a book I'd brought along. I heard the key in the lock before I'd finished the cup.

Jack is part of the Detective Division, and he usually wears a tweedy jacket to work. One thing he never looks is formal. His hair is curly and does its own thing. His pockets are stuffed with the usual things that men carry, plus his detective's notebook and some folded sheets of paper on which he doodles, thinks, and takes notes. And over on his left side, he wears a gun.

The smile that I always wait for broke as soon as he saw me. Although the first thing he does when he comes in is take off the gun and put it away, we got to each other before he had a chance, and when we wrapped our arms around each other, I could feel it against my right side. Before he'd come in, I'd had a couple of hunger pangs, but once our lips touched, once his hands caressed my back under the sweatshirt, I forgot all about food.

A long time afterward, we found the front door ajar. It made me feel good. I like a man who can forget his work sometimes.

Two weeks later I got in my car and left for Studsburg.

2

Baptism is unique among the seven sacraments. It is the only one that can be performed by a layman. It's not hard to understand why. If an unbaptized baby dies, its soul doesn't go to heaven. So if you give birth far from a Catholic community, you can perform the rite without a priest. As children we were taught how to do it.

A baptism can be performed virtually anywhere—a church, a home, an apartment. Although the church in Studsburg had not been used for decades, it was still an appropriate place for a baptism as long as it was clean and had not been desecrated. I assumed the family would take care of the former before Sunday morning.

As I drove along the southern tier of New York State, I remembered baptisms I had attended. Some were for the children of old school friends like Maddie, others for the children of former students of mine at St. Stephen's who had, for one reason or another, decided to bring their babies back to the convent for this all-important occasion. Needless to say, every baptism is a pleasure, and in this case, I was more than a little excited at the prospect of seeing a town and a church that had emerged from the deep after thirty years. To my literary soul it suggested the rebirth of the church, its symbolic baptism in the lake.

Since I normally awaken quite early, a relic of fifteen years of early morning prayers, it wasn't hard to get myself out and on the road that Saturday morning. I wanted some time to look around the town in the afternoon before the festivities got under way. Maddie had invited me to dinner at a cousin's house, so all I would have was a few hours between arriving and getting ready.

I checked into the motel and paid cash in advance for my stay. With my life-style, it'll be a long time before I qualify for a credit card. I had a strange feeling entering my room. In all my thirty years, I had never spent a night alone in a hotel. True, I had traveled, but always with another woman. On those occasions we had immediately covered the bedroom and bathroom mirrors to prevent ourselves from seeing our reflections. Today I was free of those restrictions but still near enough that I rarely lingered at a mirror.

I put my bag on the luggage rack and unpacked what needed to be hung up. As I organized the hangers, I had a surprising sense of independence. Much as I had wanted Jack to join me, something in me was glad I had come alone.

The young man at the desk gave me easy directions to Studsburg. "Just take a right out of the parking lot and go up to the first crossroad. A left for two miles, then a right at Millburg Road. I saw this morning that someone had put up a sign saying Studsburg. I think they're having some celebration at the church there tomorrow."

"A baptism," I said. "My friend's son."

"Well, that should be something to remember. That town was underwater when I was born, and I've been watching it surface for almost a year now. You going over to have a look?"

"I thought I'd like to see it before tomorrow. We'll probably all be too busy then."

"Well, if it's anything like last weekend, you may find a few cars parked near the edge of the town. They won't let you drive right into it, but you can get pretty close. The roads are pretty much gone, and the ground at the bottom is still soft. But you won't have any trouble walking around. Just don't wear high-heeled shoes."

I smiled. "I thought of that." I looked down at my sturdy sneakers. "Thank you. If anyone calls for me, tell them I'll be back by five."

"Will do. Have a nice afternoon."

The new sign that said STUDSBURG 1 MI. included a happy face, probably Maddie's doing. I turned onto the "other road" and bumped my way past a farmhouse and some cows. Beyond that, the land had an unused look and was set off from the farm by a forbidding chain-link fence. Farther along was an official-looking building with the word WATERWORKS on the sign out in front. I slowed and started to descend the immense, bowl-shaped depression that had been a reservoir. Clustered at and near the bottom were the remains of the town. A few cars were parked at what seemed to be the end of the unpaved road.

An officious-looking sign proclaimed: STUDSBURG. ENTER AT YOUR OWN RISK. I did.

I don't know what I expected, but what I saw along the easy slope down was a path already worn, and beyond it the remnants of the old town, mostly concrete foundations and, amazingly, tree stumps. If the slope had been treed, which it probably once was, it would have provided a sense of compact safety to the inhabitants. Even now there were weeds popping up along the slope, and here and there what looked like seedlings. I sometimes think in the long run vegetation will out, especially the lowest forms.

But what dominated the scene in front of me was the hollow-eyed church with its soaring steeple. I tramped through alternately dry and muddy paths, stepping occasionally on rectangles of sidewalks and chunks of streets, till I reached it. It was a classic Gothic design, shorn of windows and doors, a fairly large church for so small a community. Perhaps at one time it had drawn worshipers from nearby towns. Or more likely, perhaps the town had once known better days and a larger population.

I walked through the doorless doorway, wondering what had become of the massive doors that had once filled the emptiness. Inside, the sanctuary was stripped of anything movable, leaving a large, empty space that reminded me of descriptions of the cathedral of Chartres where once the poor camped out on a sloped floor that could easily be washed down.

Inside St. Mary Immaculate a few tourists were looking around, and several young people were sweeping away rotting debris.

"Come on in," one of them called cheerfully to me. "We're just cleaning up for tomorrow."

"What's happening tomorrow?" a woman visitor asked.

"Somebody's having a baptism."

"Here?" the woman said with disbelief.

"Yes, ma'am. Ten o'clock tomorrow morning."

"Can we come and see it?"

"Don't know why not."

I walked along the already-cleaned side of the church. There were no confessionals, but that wasn't surprising as they're often built of wood and would have been removed along with the pews. But the interior wall looked as sturdy as any I'd ever seen. Whatever material was holding the stones together looked hardly affected by three decades of water, although scattered on the walls were patches of white and green stuff that looked uncomfortably like mold.

Along the side of the sanctuary was a small room that I recognized as the sacristy, where the priest kept his vestments. It had only one window and it smelled dank and moldy. I took my trusty flashlight out of my bag, a relic of a recent time when I had needed it in an old apartment house in New York, and flashed it around the bare room. A doorway at the other end led to another room that may also have been used for storage. This one was larger and also had a second door, one that would give access to the other side of the church, where they were now cleaning up. I retraced my steps so as not to get in anyone's way and went back to the sanctuary the way I had come.

Then I went back outside, deciding to return after the baptism and wander some more. The tourists were taking pictures of the church and of the scenery, although there wasn't much to look at from an esthetic point of view. I wandered away from them off to my right, leaving church and people behind. Some distance away, an elderly couple stood together, cameraless, looking, if not bewildered, then at least full of wonder.

I raised my hand in a wave as I neared them and said, "Hi."

"Afternoon," the man said. He was wearing overalls and a plaid shirt under his jacket. "Drive up to see the town?"

"I came for a christening. My friend's son is being baptized tomorrow in St. Mary Immaculate."

He smiled and offered his hand. "You must be a friend of the Stiflers then. I'm Henry Degenkamp. This is my wife, Ellie."

"Nice to meet you. I'm Chris Bennett."

"That's the Stiflers' place right down the street there. Third house from ours." He pointed away from me down an imaginary road toward a nonexistent house. "Stiflers and Degenkamps were neighbors for generations. Kinda thought it would go on forever, but the government had other ideas."

"Was this your house?"

"Right where we're standing. Raised our kids here. That stump is where my mother planted an acorn about a hundred years ago. Hard to believe that's been underwater for thirty years."

"It is." I placed my palm on it. It felt like any stump that's been out in the sunshine for its whole life.

"You believe in miracles?"

"I'm not sure," I said, somewhat embarrassed to be caught in the midst of my own recent crisis of faith.

"Well, I don't have much longer to live—"

"Don't say that, Henry," his wife interrupted.

"—and all I ever wanted was to see my mother's oak tree and step inside that church once more. Now I've done it, I feel ready."

"You look very healthy, Mr. Degenkamp. I'm sure you have many more years ahead of you."

He patted his midsection. "Inside is where the trouble is. Can't see it from the outside."

"That's enough, Henry," his wife said.

"This must have been a wonderful place to grow up," I said, hoping to turn the conversation away from his health.

"Best place in the world, right, Ellie?"

"It was calm and peaceful and happy," she said with feeling. "There wasn't any crime, and the worst thing that happened was once in a while you'd catch a youngster smoking."

"We had a scandal, though," her husband said, his eyes twinkling.

"Henry," his wife said sharply.

"I was just going to tell her about the time the treasurer of the poker club absconded with the funds," he said smoothly.

Ellie Degenkamp smiled. "He probably didn't get enough for bus fare to New York."

"Did they ever catch him?" I asked.

"Nope. He got away with it, the son of a gun." Henry rubbed his hands together.

"It's getting chilly," his wife said.

"Then we'd best be going. We'll see you at the christening."

I watched them go, stopping as they went to point at something they saw only in memory. I walked in the direction Henry Degenkamp had pointed, toward the Stifler house. I wasn't sure where it was, but I stopped at a huge boulder, wondering if it had adorned a lawn once. Using my sneaker sole for traction, I raised myself up and sat on it. Without realizing it, I had walked up a gentle rise from the center of town. The church was near the lowest point, the houses, what was left of them, built on higher ground. But even with low buildings and tall trees, the steeple would have been visible from every part of the village. Certainly from my perch, it was.

I sat for some time thinking about the man who had absconded with the poker funds, and the kids caught smoking. In those days, the crime of smoking meant a cigarette, and the prescribed punishment a trip to the woodshed. Just sitting here made me feel transplanted to another time. Finally the chill that had made itself felt to the more sensitive bodies of the older couple got to me, too, and I jumped off the rock and started back to the hotel.

The dinner party that evening was pure pleasure. I hadn't seen Maddie's parents since I'd entered St. Stephen's fifteen years earlier, and it was nice to catch up on the intervening years. Little Richie was as good as any baby I'd ever seen, sleeping peacefully except to wake up on schedule to be nursed by his adoring mother. And Frank Clark, Maddie's husband, a nice-looking man only slightly older than the two of us, was the typical doting father. There was a lot of laughter, a lot of retelling of old stories, mostly about Studsburg, and a lot of good feeling. I left happy to be part of this warm family reunion.

3

The Stiflers had managed to track down Father Gregory Hartman, who had baptized Maddie thirty years ago, and he had agreed, without much persuasion, to come to Studsburg for the baptism of young Richard. The day was scheduled to begin at ten with a mass followed by the baptism, and go on to a lunch at the home I had visited for dinner. I intended to stay over Sunday night so that I wouldn't have to leave the festivities early.

The Degenkamps were already walking around outside the church when I arrived at nine-thirty on Sunday morning. Today they were dressed quite formally, he in a suit, she in a silk dress that peeked out from beneath her coat. We exchanged hellos and Henry said, "Come on over here, I'll show you something."

We walked away from the church, leaving his wife behind.

"Here it is." He rubbed his shoe on the earth. "See over there?" He pointed straight ahead, across the flat part of the town. "That little bridge?"

I had missed it the day before. "Was this a river?"

"A stream that ran right through the middle of town. We

used to fish it when I was a boy, not down here but over that way.'' He pointed toward the far edge of the basin. ''Trout. Every spring.''

''There isn't much left of the stream, but that bridge looks pretty sturdy.''

''That's how they built them, built everything to last. That one over there was on Main Street. Kinda narrow, but no one was in much of a hurry. If a car was coming from the other side, you just waited your turn.''

''Come on, Henry,'' Mrs. Degenkamp called. ''I want to sit where I can see what's going on.''

''We're coming,'' he called back, and together we went into the church.

The Stiflers and Clarks had had several rows of chairs and kneeling pads placed in the front of the church, and two young men were making sure that only invited guests had first choice. A number of visitors clustered in the rear, and several people had already found seats up front. The priest was shaking hands with a few in the front row, an unexpected reunion. Maddie had told me that a number of former Studsburgers had been invited, her mother and grandmother having kept up with them. There were more than the usual number of gray heads and more than the usual exclamations of surprise as people recognized one another.

I waited at the side till Maddie entered the church, then joined her. Frank insisted I sit in the first row with them, and I did so happily. As we approached, the Degenkamps looked around and stood to hug and kiss the Stiflers and then ooh and ahh over Maddie and her baby. The last time they had seen Maddie, she was the size of little Richie.

Promptly at ten, without benefit of music, Father Hartman began the mass. When it concluded, Richard Clark in his magnificent white christening dress was baptized a Catholic.

Father Hartman came to the luncheon and regaled us with tales of Studsburg as it once was. He had spent only six years in the town and was now, I estimated, in his late sixties, a tall, good-looking man with graying hair and dark eyes. To hear him tell it, those were the six best years of his life. In fact, to hear any of them tell it, Studsburg was the kind of town you could only love. It was a place of contentment, a town where people knew and trusted one another.

At some point during the afternoon, Maddie's cousin hauled out an old photograph album and passed it around. There in black and white was the last day of Studsburg's official existence, the Fourth of July, the christening day of Madeleine Stifler Clark, wearing the very same dress her son was wearing today. When the book was finally passed to me, I turned the pages slowly, identifying young Father Hartman, the Degenkamps in their fifties, not their eighties, Maddie's cousins, her mother, almost a wisp of a girl. All were seated at picnic tables somewhere outside the church. The woman sitting next to me on the sofa kept looking over, pointing out faces and attaching names to them. Further along there were snapshots of fireworks as the town celebrated its final moments and the birth of their country. When I was finished, I noticed that the crowd was thinning. It was late afternoon.

I passed along the album and stood. Mrs. Stifler told me Maddie was upstairs nursing the baby, and I found her in a bedroom.

"This is wonderful, Maddie," I said, sitting on the edge of the bed.

"Don't tell me you're leaving. I won't let you."

"I want to get a last look at Studsburg before I go. It could start to rain tomorrow and the whole town could be underwater by summer."

"Come back and see us tonight, Kix. I've hardly had a chance to talk to you."

"OK."

"Promise?"

"Yes, I promise. This was such a wonderful idea, Maddie. I hope Richie gets to see St. Mary Immaculate when he's old enough to appreciate it."

Maddie smiled and touched the little face with her finger. "It's been a little overwhelming," she admitted, "but I'm

glad we did it. Go," she ordered. "And don't forget to come
back."

There was only one car parked at the edge of the town
when I got there, a beat-up old blue something-or-other. The
afternoon had become cold and I was a little sorry I hadn't
gone back to the hotel to change but I wanted to see the town
while there was still a remnant of daylight. I pulled my shoes
off and put on the sneakers I had had in the car all day. Then
I started for the church.

The chairs had all been removed and the sanctuary was
clean and empty. Usually when I visit a church I light three
candles, for my mother, my father, and my Aunt Meg. I was
sorry I hadn't thought ahead and brought some, but at that
moment, a gust of wind blew through the windowless open-
ings, chilling me and letting me know my candles would not
have survived.

I walked around the left side where the boys had been
cleaning yesterday and found the door to the priest's sacristy
as I had anticipated. Just outside it was a curving flight of
stone steps leading, I supposed, to the basement. I took my
flashlight out of my bag and started down. The dank, fishy
smell was more pronounced and I almost turned back, but
the knowledge that this was the only chance I would have to
see it kept me going. There was debris on the stairs and I
walked carefully, shining the light just enough ahead that I
could see my way.

At the bottom, a low-ceilinged hall ran to my right, curving along the rear of the building. Almost immediately I
came to a doorway. From the little light that entered through
the high windows, I could tell this was the hall where meetings and bingo games took place. Like the upstairs, it had
been stripped of the stage that would have been built at one
end. The floor here was slimy underfoot, and I walked carefully back to the hallway. Suddenly I heard a little ping, as
though something small like a coin had fallen on the concrete

floor. I stopped and flashed my light farther ahead, but I couldn't see much because of the curve of the building.

"Hello," I called. "Anyone there?"

In answer, I heard a metallic clatter, as though someone were gathering up tools, and then the footsteps of someone running.

"Who's there?" I called. But the footsteps were already hurriedly mounting the stairs at the far end of the hall. I kept walking. I passed another doorway, probably the furnace room. I raised my flashlight and saw the stone stairs along the far wall. Lowering the beam, I spotted something on the floor near the interior wall that supported the stairs. It looked like one of the rectangular stones that formed the walls down here. I wondered if it had become loose from thirty years underwater.

But it didn't appear that way. There were chunks of mortar on the ground around the stone, as though someone had just dug it out. When I had nearly reached it, my light caught something gold on the floor. I picked it up and pocketed it. Then I sat on my heels and pointed the flashlight into the opening under the stairs.

I drew in my breath and said, "Oh no," and at the same moment, I crossed myself.

Inside the exposed opening, dirty and fleshless, was all that remained of a body that had been underwater for three decades.

4

It was surely the first time in a long time that Studsburg had seen flashing lights and tan uniforms. I had had to go back to the motel to find a telephone, and after calling the police, I telephoned Maddie to tell her what happened. When I got back to the church, Mr. and Mrs. Stifler were just arriving.

Mrs. Stifler looked frightened. "Maddie said you found a body, Kix. Is it someone we know? A guest of ours?"

"I think it's someone who was killed before Studsburg was flooded," I said. "I'd better find the police. They'll want to know how I found it." I excused myself and went into the church.

It was the sheriff's department that had responded to my call, and deputies had already cordoned off the two stairways with long strips of yellow plastic bearing the ongoing inscription CRIME SCENE DO NOT CROSS, but the man at the top of one let me through when I identified myself. At the foot of the stairs, two uniformed men were on the floor peering into the opening in the wall.

"I'm Christine Bennett," I said. "I called in the report."

"Deputy Drago," one of the men said, rising to his feet. "Thanks for dropping by. I'd like to write down anything you can tell me while it's fresh in your mind."

I retraced my brief walk down the far stairs, into the meeting room, and down the hall, recalling the sound of tools clanging and of running footsteps.

"Man or woman?" he asked.

"I didn't see, but if I had to guess, I'd say a man. It sounded kind of heavy. It certainly wasn't a woman in heels."

"That's a pretty heavy stone for a woman to move. So you didn't see him at all?"

"Not even a shadow. He must have heard me—" I looked down at my sneakers and shook my head "—or maybe he saw the beam of my flashlight. No, wait a minute. I heard him and I called hello."

"He answer?"

"No, he ran."

"You always carry a flashlight?" he asked.

I took it out of my bag. It was small and lightweight. "I need it sometimes at night."

"You touch anything there?"

"Nothing. I just got down to look in the opening, and then I got up and left to call you."

He looked down at his notes. "You said there was a car parked at the edge of the town when you got there. Was it still there when you left?"

"It was gone."

"Did the person you heard go up the stairs have enough time to get to a car while you were down here?"

I had thought of that on my way over. "I don't think so, but I'm not sure."

"You didn't by any chance see or hear the car leave, did you?"

"No, I didn't."

"So this guy could've left on foot, and some other person might have been walking around town while you were down here."

"It's possible."

"Which means three people could have been here at the same time, not two."

"That's right. It's even possible that whoever was down here didn't leave right away. It was getting dark, and there are probably plenty of little nooks and crannies right in the church where he could have hidden."

The deputy thought it over. "And left after you drove away."

"Either that or he could still be here." The Stiflers weren't the only ones who had arrived. Someone hiding in the church or outside in the shadows could easily merge with a group arriving by car.

"We did a pretty thorough search upstairs when we got here," Deputy Drago said. "No pews for him to hide under anymore. Outside's another story."

While we were talking, the photographer had arrived and was busy taking pictures on his hands and knees. Although the opening in the wall was just as I had left it, I had avoided looking into it.

"Do you suppose that body's been there for thirty years?" I asked now.

"Gotta be," the deputy said. "This is the first time anyone's seen this town since it was flooded. I grew up knowing it as a lake."

"It must have seemed like such a safe place to bury someone," I mused.

"You're right about that," he agreed. "This was no spur-of-the-moment murder. It must've taken a lot of work to get that stone loose, then get the body down here and seal it up again." He closed his notebook and stuck his pen back in his pocket. "It'll be a bitch to figure out, I can tell you. I don't envy the county coroner this one. That body's little more than a pile of bones."

"I know." An hour ago when I had gotten down to look inside the opening, the first thing I'd seen was a skeletal hand protruding slightly, as though it had rested on the stone and then dropped into the space the stone had occupied when it was moved.

"Hey, Tony?" someone called.

"Right here," Deputy Drago said.

"We're to take it to the hospital morgue. The coroner's in Buffalo visiting his daughter. Be back tomorrow morning."

"OK with me. You finished yet, Gary?" he asked the photographer.

The man with the camera got up off the floor, his clothes dirty from the drying muck. He brushed them carelessly. "I'll need some more shots when you get it out, but you can move it now if you want."

"The coroner's people here yet?" Deputy Drago asked.

"On their way," the other uniform said.

They came down the stairs as he finished speaking. When they saw the remains—I couldn't really think of that mass of bones as a body—they groaned and swore.

"Damn thing's gonna fall apart when we move it," one of them said. He looked at the stretcher and shook his head. "What we need for this one is a plastic bag."

Drago walked over to them. "Keep your eyes open for any jewelry that could identify him. I don't know how the hell anyone's gonna figure this one out."

The man holding the stretcher laughed. "You can crawl in there when we're done and have a look."

"Thanks," Drago said sarcastically. "You can bet I will."

"Hey, Tony," the man with the stretcher said. "There's a sneaker in here. Look at this." He pulled a dirt-encrusted shoe out of the opening and scratched his fingernail over the back of it. "Keds! Can you beat that?"

Drago looked at it, then turned around and saw me. "Look, Miss Bennett, you may as well go. If we have any more questions, we can call your hotel."

"Fine."

"And thanks for your cooperation."

I took a piece of paper out of my bag and scribbled my name and home telephone number on it. "I'd appreciate it if you'd let me know what the coroner finds out. I mean, if he has any idea who it is."

"Sure thing. But I wouldn't expect too much from this one. If someone had reported this guy missing thirty years ago, it'd be one thing. But I have a feeling this is a John Doe that's gonna end up in potter's field."

"You will check the records from back then, won't you?"

"You can count on it." He smiled. "Good night now."

I said good night and went up the far stairs.

The Stiflers were still in the church near the front door, where the police were holding back the curious. They looked very unhappy, and I went over to talk to them and reassure them that there was no connection between today's baptism and the gruesome discovery in the basement. They seemed to feel responsible, as though in some way today's celebration had caused the discovery.

"I just can't believe it," Mrs. Stifler said. "Do they know who it is?"

"No idea at all."

"How terrible." She shook her head.

"Let's get back," her husband said. "Maddie'll be having fits."

I smiled as we left the church. If anyone in this world is together, it's Maddie Clark. The day she has fits is the day the world falls apart.

"Come back to the house, Kix," Mr. Stifler said. "Let's all have a cup of coffee and calm down."

It sounded like a good idea, and I followed them in my car. When Maddie heard the story, her eyes lit up. "Fun," she said with the kind of excitement I remembered from years ago. "I get baptized and someone gets knocked off. Are we missing any relatives, Mom?"

"Maddie, really," Mrs. Stifler said with quiet exasperation, making me smile. They had learned to get along with each other, but Maddie still provoked the old feelings in her mother.

"How many people were at Maddie's christening?" I asked when we had sat down with coffee mugs and a plate of tempting cakes left over from the afternoon's celebration.

"Forty, would you say?" Maddie's father said, looking at his wife.

"Just about."

"I had the feeling the whole town had been invited."

"Well, they were, but most of them had left by then,"
Mrs. Stifler said. "Some more came in the evening for the
fireworks, people who had moved in the area. We were supposed to be out of Studsburg by the last of June, but the
middle of June came and I hadn't given birth yet, and that
nice colonel in the Army Corps of Engineers was very sympathetic. And besides, everyone wanted to celebrate the
Fourth in Studsburg. What was his name, Harry?"

"Uh . . . Wright, I think."

"Yes, Colonel Wright. That's it. He was a nice young
man, and his own wife had had a baby not long before, and
he sympathized with my problem. We had our new house
already, but it was far away and I wanted my own doctor and
the hospital I was used to, and Father Hartman for the baptism. Colonel Wright said a few days one way or the other
wouldn't matter."

"We'd all known about this move for a year," Harry Stifler added. "And a lot of people just wanted to get out and
get on with their lives. So they'd already moved away."

"But some who stayed in the area came back for the christening, Harry. The Rogerses? Remember?"

"That's right. And the Davidsons. They're all in the pictures, Kix, everyone who was there."

Mrs. Stifler turned toward me suddenly with a dark look.
"You don't think that one of our guests killed that poor soul
in the church basement, Kix, do you?"

"I don't know," I said honestly. "But it must have been
someone familiar with Studsburg, someone who could walk
around and not be singled out as a stranger."

"No one in that town was a stranger," Harry Stifler said.
"I grew up there and I knew everyone, even the peculiar old
birds that kept to themselves. When I married Carol, she
moved into my parents' house until we could afford a place
of our own. We found out pretty quick that Maddie was
coming along, and right about then we heard what they were

going to do with the town, so it made sense to look for work somewhere else, which I did.''

''How many of the old Studsburgers did you keep in touch with?'' I asked.

''Oh, lots of them,'' Carol Stifler said. ''We had a round-robin letter for about ten years until it petered out, and I had a huge Christmas card list. Several of the old people went to old-age homes, and others went to live with their families, I remember. That reduced the list a little. I still keep in touch with a lot of them, you know. Like the Degenkamps. They must have been about our age thirty years ago, don't you think, Harry?''

''Just about.''

Carol Stifler laughed nervously. ''I really don't think old Henry Degenkamp murdered anyone, Kix.''

But, of course, that was exactly the trouble when you knew all the possible suspects. They were all so *nice*. They were all your friends. You'd trusted them with your problems, your children, perhaps even your money. ''I don't either,'' I said. ''Anyway, I'm sure the sheriff's people will take care of it.''

The truth was, I thought the sheriff's office probably wouldn't take care of it. There had been such a casual attitude in the treatment of the remains, and Deputy Drago was pretty skeptical about the coroner turning up any useful information from an autopsy. What they had found, Deputy Drago had said, was little more than ''a pile of bones.''

It hurt and troubled me. After I'd had my coffee and the requisite piece of cake, I said good night and drove back to the motel. During the drive I kept thinking about the person, the soul, if you will, that had inhabited the pile of bones in the church basement. He had been a living, breathing person, and his life had been taken from him deliberately by a killer who had schemed cleverly, either killing him and dragging his body to the church basement or luring the unsuspecting victim down there to be killed. Whoever he was, he deserved better.

5

I parked my car and walked through the front entrance of the motel.

"Christine," someone said in a surprised voice, and I turned to find Father Hartman beside me.

"Hello, Father. I didn't know you were staying here, too."

"Have you heard what happened?" he asked.

"Yes. I'm afraid I'm the one who found the body. I've just given a statement to the police."

"It's all over the news. Do they have any idea who it is?"

"Not unless they found some identification after I left. I kind of doubt that they will. Thirty years underwater hasn't left much to identify."

"Come and join me for a drink," he said. We were standing not far from the bar.

"Thank you, I'd like that."

He ordered a Scotch on the rocks, and I asked for a glass of dry sherry. We sat at a small table designed more for intimate couples than an ex-nun and a graying priest nearing retirement.

"They said on the news flash that the body had been found in the church basement." His face showed his undisguised distaste.

"Someone had chiseled out a stone in the wall supporting the stairs. The body was inside. I think it could have stayed hidden forever if the killer hadn't gone looking for it. I've been trying to figure out why he came back after all these years."

''Maybe to reassure himself that the body was still there and wouldn't be discovered by the tourists that are visiting Studsburg these days.''

''He could have seen that just by looking at that stone wall. Maybe there was some identification in there that he wanted to retrieve, or maybe he just couldn't keep away from the scene of his crime.''

''They say that about killers,'' Father Hartman said.

''I wonder when it happened,'' I mused.

''What do you mean?''

''Well, the body's been underwater for thirty years, but we don't really know when the murder happened. That's an old church, isn't it?''

''Very old.''

''The person could have been killed forty or fifty years ago, or even more.''

''Yes, you're right. I hadn't thought of that.'' The priest frowned, looking thoughtful. After a moment he shook his head. ''No, I'm afraid you're not right, Chris. It couldn't have happened before I came to Studsburg.''

''How do you know?''

''Because after I'd been there a couple of years—I really can't pinpoint the date—we noticed some disintegration in those supporting walls under both stairways, and I had them completely rebuilt. I can assure you there was nothing under those stairs. Certainly there wasn't a body.''

''That narrows it down then, doesn't it?''

''Substantially. And let me say something else. I'm a priest. I was in my church every day. I was everywhere in that church. I would surely have noticed a moved stone in the basement or fresh concrete or whatever they use to hold those stones together. If it happened during my tenure, it happened at the end.''

''It must be hard to think of someone in your parish as a killer,'' I said.

''They were all good people, hard workers, the best of neighbors. I've never had a parish I liked better.''

"Maybe it wasn't a member of the parish," I said. "If there were army men around those last months, one of them could have done it."

"I suppose that's a possibility," he said thoughtfully.

"But you don't think so." I could see the idea troubled him.

"The army wasn't there the last few days. They finished their work at the end of June. The whole town was empty and very quiet those first days of July. There were only a handful of Studsburgers left in their homes."

At that moment I really had not thought of getting involved in the investigation. At home I had a class that I taught; in New York I had the work I did for Arnold Gold; in my personal life I had Jack Brooks. But I couldn't deny my curiosity. "Do you remember the last days of Studsburg, Father Hartman?" I asked.

"With great clarity, as I'm sure most of the residents would. You're not likely to live through two such occasions in one lifetime."

"I noticed that the interior of the church had been stripped bare. When was that done?"

"While we were still there. The army extended our stay to the Fourth of July to accommodate the young Stifler couple, who were expecting their first child—but of course, you know them."

"I went to high school with Maddie."

"I see. But they worked, the army, that is, till the end of June as scheduled to prepare for the eventual flooding of the village. All that was left in the church that last day was my cassock. The congregation stood during the mass because the pews had been taken out about a week earlier. I bought one, by the way, and took it to my next parish as a memento."

"So did Mrs. Stifler. I remember seeing it when Maddie and I went to her house. What I'm really asking is, could someone have buried a body in the church before the day of Maddie's christening?"

He shook his head slowly. "I don't see how. The men working there were around all the time."

"But not at night. A soldier could have come back at night."

"True, true." He thought about it. "But they were billeted some distance away, and bused in and out. Getting from the barracks to the church—with a body—I just can't see how that could have been done. And as I said, I was in the church every day. I was watching the army's progress even though I wasn't officially overseeing it."

"What about after the Fourth?"

"We were out of there. That was the agreement, and as far as I know, everyone adhered to it. There weren't that many people left anyway. All the stores had already closed, and most of Main Street had been bulldozed. I had my bags packed and I left the day after the christening, I'd say along about noon."

"Do you remember if you said good-bye to the others?"

"To all of them. They all seemed to drop by the rectory on their way out of town. It was very emotional."

"I'm sure it must have been."

"Well, we seem to have narrowed down when this killing happened."

"Not that it matters," I said. "But if it couldn't have taken place before the christening and if the army got everyone out the next day, then it must have happened on the Fourth of July, day or night."

"Oh, they got us all out on schedule. I didn't stay around the area, but several parishioners wrote to me, and some of them described the wire fences the army put up to keep people out while they bulldozed and cleaned up. Knowing the army, I wouldn't be surprised if they kept a guard there at night."

It sounded logical to me, too. "I know there was a picnic after the baptism," I said.

"Oh yes, a great celebration in the yard behind the church."

"Then people must have gone in and out of the church to use the bathroom or get water."

He looked thoughtful. "Why do I think they didn't?" he asked out loud. And then, almost immediately, he came up with the answer. "They'd already shut off the water in the church and taken out the plumbing. No, no one went into the church after the baptism, not that I could see anyway. They used the bathroom and the kitchen in the rectory that day."

"And where was the rectory?"

"Right behind the church. I used to go in through the back door."

"That must be near the stairs to the basement."

"Right next to one set of stairs, yes."

But someone could easily have walked away from the group and gone into the church through the front door, which was completely hidden from the view of the picnickers. Which led me back to the uncomfortable assumption that one of the guests at the baptism had been a killer, and another had been a victim.

I decided not to pursue it any further. Surely the Stiflers would have known if one of their guests disappeared. And that Christmas card list Carol Stifler had mentioned—someone on that list would have let her know that a husband, wife, parent, or child had dropped from sight. It wasn't worth thinking about.

"Tell me, Father, how is it that the army didn't bulldoze the church along with all the other buildings in Studsburg?"

"That was due entirely to the intervention of the bishop."

"How interesting."

"St. Mary Immaculate was one of the oldest Catholic churches in the state. As you saw this morning, it wasn't all that big, but it was architecturally very fine, a graceful building. When the bishop heard that it was going to be razed along with everything else in Studsburg, he flew into a rage. There were stories in the local papers, debates, speeches. That was before the time of sit-ins and demonstrations, but a lot of people, not just parishioners, agreed with the bishop."

"And the army gave in?"

"They sent some engineers out to look the building over, and they decided it was sturdily built and probably wouldn't crumble underwater. We had to agree to strip the inside of anything made of wood or fabric, but that was a small price to pay. He was quite a man, Bishop O'Rourke," Father Hartman said, his eyes narrowing and a little smile playing on his lips. "I believe he said once that the day would come when the church would rise again. At the time I thought he meant it metaphorically."

I felt a chill course through me. "It seems he was right."

"You know, when I heard the level of the lake had dropped and the cross at the top of the steeple was visible, I drove down here one day to see it."

"I can understand why. It's an amazing thing to have happened. Bishop O'Rourke isn't alive anymore, is he?"

"Not for many years. I think he felt that preserving that church was the culmination of a life's work."

My glass was empty, and the ice in Father Hartman's was half-melted. "I ought to get upstairs," I said. "I have a long trip tomorrow."

"The Stiflers told me you used to be a Franciscan sister."

"I was. I left my convent last spring."

"I'm sorry to hear that. We seem to lose so many of the best these days."

"It was a decision I reached over a long time with a lot of soul-searching."

"I'm sure it was," he said with a smile, but I knew I represented a loss to him, a loss to the church.

I was really too tired to talk about it, so I said good night and went up to my room.

"Yeah—hello," Jack's voice said, his weariness audible.

"It's me. Still hitting the books?"

"Oh, hi, Chris. Yeah, I'm knee-deep. I'll probably take a sleep break soon. I'm glad you called."

"I may leave a little later tomorrow than I planned. Something crazy's happened." I told him, listened to his amazed response. We talked for a few minutes more and I heard him loosen up. I could see him at his desk in the room that was his entire apartment minus the small bedroom. I had been lucky in so many ways to find him, luckier still that he had been the first man in my life. The thought of going out with many men, of building small relationships with accompanying intimacies and seeing them dashed for whatever reasons men and women fail to come together, was very daunting to me. Jack had simply been there, not as a potential suitor, which might at that time have terrified me, but as a source of information and help. That we had become lovers was still a wonder to me.

By the time we hung up, he sounded wide-awake, more interested in the thirty-year-old murder than the test the next night. I told him to forget the murder, and I tried to do the same. I wasn't exactly successful.

It made the front page of the local morning newspaper on Monday. I was mentioned and had the distinction of seeing my last name misspelled. Maddie called early and asked me to drop over before leaving. First I had a leisurely breakfast. Father Hartman was nowhere around, and I was sorry I hadn't said a more formal good-bye the night before.

With only one small bag to pack, I was ready to check out a little after nine. I turned in my key at the desk and went out to my car.

Something drew me back to Studsburg. I knew there was nothing to see, that the police wouldn't let anyone into that church until they were satisfied they had scraped up every crumb of evidence, and that might take some time considering the condition of the opening under the stairs. But I drove there anyway.

Two sheriff's cars were parked outside the church. I left

mine at the edge of the town and walked down the slope. I was dressed to be comfortable for several hours of driving, jeans and flannel shirt under my coat. As this was my first fall and winter out of the convent, I had not yet acquired a winter jacket to go with the pants that I wear when I'm home. I live happily on a small income that is many times what I lived on during the fifteen years I spent at St. Stephen's. You can survive winter easily without a jacket as long as you have a warm coat, and you need a coat when you go to work in New York.

"This is a crime scene, ma'am," a tall, weathered, uniformed man informed me as I approached the church.

"I wondered if the body had been identified yet," I said.

"No word on that. The coroner's doing an autopsy sometime today. You aren't the lady who found the body, are you?"

"I am."

"They get your name right in the paper?"

"No, but it doesn't matter." I smiled, and he smiled back.

"Well, there isn't much I can tell you right now except I can't let anyone in the church."

"Do you mind if I walk around the town?"

"Be my guest."

I started off for the little bridge Henry Degenkamp had pointed out to me Sunday morning. The land was flat here, the old riverbed a slight running indentation. I stepped into it and felt a small difference in texture, a gritty sandiness. Off to my right, the once residential area of Studsburg sloped upward. I saw where I had been on Saturday afternoon, the place where I had met the Degenkamps.

Ahead of me, the little bridge he had pointed out yesterday morning was now quite close. Reaching it, I had a sense of how narrow the river had been at this point, and how narrow, too, the street that crossed it. It was a beautiful old bridge. I took hold of one side and lifted myself up onto it. It felt as sturdy and stable as any country bridge that still handled traffic.

From the center of the bridge I turned in a full circle. This was Main Street where on both sides there had been shops that supported life, probably a grocery, a gas station, a coffee shop, a bank. Looking up Main Street as it rose along the hill, I could see two perfect rows of tree stumps. It had been a town that cared how it looked, even if no one saw it but its own, a group of people who remembered their friends with round-robin letters and Christmas cards, some of whom returned after thirty years for a baptism in the old church. But among them there had been a cold-blooded killer who had planned his crime and executed it virtually in plain view of the townspeople.

I jumped down off the bridge and started back toward the church, wondering what terrible event, what anger, what resentment, had motivated a mortal crime. Love, money, jealousy, or something so terrible that I could not imagine it.

The deputy waved to me as I passed on my way to my car.

"Gosh, I'm sorry you missed Frank," Maddie said when I had taken off my coat. "He had to get back to work, so he took off at five this morning. I'll be leaving after lunch. Then Richie can sleep as we drive. Mom tells me your name was in the paper this morning."

"All I did was find the body," I said. "I hope the coroner figures out pretty quick who he was."

"It just can't have been a Studsburger," Carol Stifler said. "Harry and I went over and over it last night. *Nobody* was missing after Maddie's christening. The mayor even dittoed address lists and gave them to everyone in town. If somebody had disappeared, the post office would have sent a Christmas card back or I would have gotten a note saying so-and-so was gone. Nothing like that happened."

"Well, whoever it is, he's stirring up quite a dispute right now between the coroner and the sheriff," her husband said.

"What kind of dispute?" I asked. I hadn't turned on the television set in my room this morning, so all I had was the morning paper, which had nothing new in it.

"They're both just basking in the glory of your discovery, Kix. I expect the sheriff's going to parlay this murder into a windfall for his department. And the coroner the same. He's on his way back from Buffalo with a team of reporters at his heels. They both seem to be enjoying the limelight."

I felt disgusted. "I just hope they do their jobs."

"In their own sweet time, I expect. They have nothing to gain by hurrying."

"Do you have pictures of Studsburg as it used to look?" I asked.

"Tons of them," Carol Stifler said. "But I didn't bring them with me. If you want to see them, come on over someday and we'll sit down together. Harry and I still live in the same house we had when you and Maddie were in school."

"Maybe I'll give you a call."

"I can see this has unsettled you, dear."

It had, and I was even more unsettled at the prospect of seeing two county officials try to enhance their public offices at the expense of some poor soul who was dead. "It certainly hasn't dimmed the happiness of this occasion," I assured her. "I wish I could stay longer, but I have to be on my way. Maybe I'll call you and we'll look at those pictures."

"It would be my pleasure."

We all hugged and kissed, and the cousin in whose house we were gave me a care package with enough party leftovers to keep me eating the rest of the week. Maddie walked me out to the car, and we gave each other a final squeeze. Then I took off.

6

When I gave Deputy Drago my phone number, I foolishly expected him to call me and tell me what he had learned from the autopsy. Looking back as I stuffed myself that evening with goodies from the baptism celebration, I knew my optimism had been rather naive. As far as Deputy Drago was concerned, I was nothing more than the person who had accidentally discovered the body. I was not on his list, long or short, of people to be briefed.

I was pretty sure the coroner would have completed his autopsy sometime that day, and equally sure that the sheriff's department would know the results. When I finished eating, I called the sheriff's office. Deputy Drago was there, and he came on the line when he heard my name.

"What can I do for you?" he asked cordially.

"I wondered if the body had been identified."

"Well, it hasn't been, but we've gotten a little surprise. It wasn't a he. It's the body of a woman."

"A woman!"

"That's right. The coroner estimates she'd have been in her twenties, possibly early thirties, about five six, and probably weighed a hundred twenty or a hundred twenty-five pounds. Well built. And the coroner's pretty sure she wasn't pregnant."

"How can he know all that if there isn't much besides bones?"

"Well, partly from the bone structure. She was wearing a pair of men's Levi's, and from the size of the hips, he figures she was a well-proportioned woman. And her sneakers were a woman's size seven.''

''Was there a purse or wallet in that opening?'' I asked.

''Nothing that could identify her. No rings, no jewelry, nothing. The coroner's sending X rays of her teeth to all the local dentists in the area, but we're not too optimistic. If she went to one, he might be dead now, and who knows what happened to his files?''

''Was there a dentist in Studsburg?''

''Didn't seem to be. The sheriff knew the town pretty well when he was younger. Said there weren't any doctors or anything like that. Folks used to go to another town for that kind of stuff.''

''Do you know how she died?'' I asked.

''She was shot. We found the bullet in the silt on the floor, a typical round-nosed lead bullet like the ones they used back in the fifties and sixties. Comes from a .38-caliber revolver. It works well up close, but it's kind of inaccurate at distances. She was shot pretty close. The bullet doesn't mean much, though. Lots of folks around here have a handgun.''

''What about missing persons?'' I asked, reaching for my last straw.

''I checked that out myself, Miss Bennett. Just doesn't seem to have been any reported around that time. We don't get a lot of missing-person reports around here, and the ones we get, they usually show up later on their own.''

I sighed. ''So it's kind of a dead end,'' I said.

''Looks like it.''

''Deputy Drago, Studsburg had a mayor. I don't know who he was or where he moved to, but he would probably know everyone who lived in town. And the priest, Father Hartman. I'm sure he'd remember everyone in his parish. Or he'd know where the records are kept.''

''Right you are, ma'am. We're a pretty modern office up here, and we're looking into everything, I promise you.''

''I'm sure you are. I didn't mean to imply that you

weren't.'' I felt a little guilty. Sometimes when you have a connection to the New York Police Department, it's easy to feel that any other law enforcement group is inferior. I hoped he wouldn't feel insulted.

''So you just let us do our job, and if anything turns up, I'm sure you'll hear about it.''

I thanked him and hung up. I didn't think I'd hear about anything without a prod.

I stayed downstairs till ten and watched the news on several channels. Sure enough, the story had reached New York. Standing before a large seal, and flanked by the American flag and some other flag I didn't recognize, the coroner appeared in a brief clip announcing the surprising finding that the mystery body was that of a young woman. Lights flashed as he spoke, and seemed to infuse him with spirit. He was a rotund man with jowls and little left of his hair, but his pleasure at being in the spotlight was evident.

In a separate, briefer clip, the sheriff, in full regalia, announced that a thorough search had begun to learn the identity of the body, starting with dental records. And, I thought sadly, probably ending with them.

I taught my class on Poetry and the Contemporary American Woman on Tuesday morning and then drove home, thinking about the woman. What if she had a perfect set of teeth and had never seen a dentist? What if the records were gone? How could a young woman so anger someone that he would kill her?

Besides the possibility of identification through dental records, there was one other thing in favor of discovering the woman's identity. If anyone in the area remembered a young woman missing thirty years ago, all the publicity would surely awaken those memories. Perhaps it was best to wait and see what happened.

Jack called Tuesday evening when he got home. ''Not bad,'' he said when I asked him about the test. ''Just a hell

of a lot of work studying for it. I really needed yesterday.
You get that upstate murder solved yet?''

"I have not yet begun to investigate," I paraphrased, "and
I probably won't.''

"If I know you, you're champing at the bit to dig into
some old files.''

"I wouldn't even know what files to look for, Jack. The
sheriff's office is sending X rays of the woman's teeth to local
dentists, but I wouldn't be surprised if that's a dead end after
so many years. And Maddie's parents are sure no one from
Studsburg was missing after Maddie's baptism. So if it wasn't
a Studsburger, how are we ever going to put a name on her?''

"You'll think of a way," he said lightly.

"The truth is, I'm troubled that the coroner and the sheriff
are using this to promote themselves. I keep imagining this
poor dead girl as a person, someone who had something to
do with Studsburg and met her death there, a violent, planned
death.''

"That's the way sheriffs and coroners act, honey. They
don't live exciting lives like mine, so they—'' My laughter
stopped him. "You making fun of my exciting life?''

"Just enjoying the image. Listen to me, Jack. Suppose the
day I left St. Stephen's, someone had stopped my car and
killed me and hidden the body. No one in Oakwood would
miss me, because no one knew me and no one knew I was
coming.''

"Your friend Sister Joseph would call, and eventually,
when she couldn't find you, she'd report you missing.''

"Suppose I left the convent in anger.''

"OK. I get your point.''

"And thirty years later some kids pull a rock away from
a cave along the Hudson, and there are my bones. I had no
family to worry about me. Maybe I had no job to go to.
There are people like that, Jack!''

"I get the drift. There are some holes—like the fact that
you own a house and have to pay taxes on it—but yes, it

could be that kind of person. So what was she doing in the basement of that church with a killer?''

''I wish I knew.''

''And your friend's parents said no one was missing.''

''Either they're wrong or the woman wasn't a Studsburger.''

''I knew you weren't going to let this alone,'' he said.

''She deserves a decent burial, Jack. I think I'll just go over that list Mrs. Stifler has.''

''Can you squeeze me in this weekend?''

''You bet.''

If the body was still news upstate, it certainly wasn't in New York. It had been good for about ninety seconds of TV notoriety, and now it was gone. I went out for an early walk on Wednesday morning, hoping to think the situation through, but I met my neighbor Melanie Gross, and we walked and talked together.

''Any chance Hal and I can meet the boyfriend?'' she asked. I had told her about Jack a couple of weeks earlier. ''Or are you keeping him all to yourself?''

''I'd love you to meet him.''

''How about dinner at our place some weekend?''

''Fine. I'll talk to him when I see him Saturday, and we'll get together on a date.''

We speeded up a bit—Mel is a runner and I'm a walker, so a little cooperation and compromise are necessary in our friendship—and talked about town politics, an almost endless source of conversation and not a little sniping. When we got back to Pine Brook Road, Mel left me at my driveway and continued on to her own. I went inside and made myself breakfast. If I called Deputy Drago, he would have every right to be annoyed. But I knew I wasn't going to get a call from him unless he had specific information that would identify the victim. I sat with my coffee, trying to justify my involvement in a case that was none of my business. She wasn't a friend or a relative of the Stiflers. In all probability, she wasn't even a Studsburger. There was a good likelihood she wasn't a Catholic. The killer had just chosen the church because it was the only building that wouldn't be destroyed by the Army Corps of Engineers, and everyone who lived in the town knew that.

She was nothing to me, just an unfortunate person who had met her death in the basement of St. Mary Immaculate thirty years ago. My only connection to her was a coincidence, that I had meandered through the church at the same time that her killer had returned to view his handiwork.

I finished my coffee and went to the phone. The county coroner was too busy or too unimpressed with my name and lack of credentials to answer my call. Someone else spoke to me, a woman with a gentle manner and an upstate edge to her speech. She assured me the coroner was doing *everything* he could to find the killer of the young lady. When I pressed her on what everything amounted to, I got what was apparently the party line: There had been an autopsy, and the coroner had "gone public" to see if anyone "out there" had some knowledge of the deceased.

In other words, he'd done the minimum required of his job, and he'd had a little free publicity besides. That put him in the same corner as the sheriff. Ordinarily I try not to be judgmental, but it looked as though both departments had pretty much given up. If something dropped in their laps, they might act on it, but there wasn't going to be any aggressive investigation. No one had reported her missing thirty years ago. No one cared then, no one cared now. She was a pile of bones that had been dumped in a basement wall.

When I got off the phone, I went back to the kitchen table. I sat facing the window to the backyard. Today it was a bleak wintry gray. That girl might have been my mother's age. Were she alive today, she might have a large family, including grandchildren. We had talked about John Donne yesterday in my poetry class, and a line flitted through my head: "Every man's death diminishes me because I am involved in mankind."

What other connection did I need?

* * *

"This was our house," Carol Stifler said, the photo album half on her lap, half on mine. "Really my in-laws' house, but we had nowhere else to live when we were married, and Harry was afraid to commit himself until we could afford it. We were very careful with money in those days."

"It's a pretty house," I said.

"It was built around the turn of the century. I guess it'd be about a hundred years old now. Seems a pity, doesn't it?"

I said something in agreement. She had been pleased to get my phone call this morning, and I had driven over for lunch and a session with the album. The pictures were moving slowly, because each one evoked memories and conversation. "The Degenkamps said they lived just down the street."

"Yes, they did. I have a picture of their house somewhere. Oh, here it is."

"That must be the tree they told me about."

"Studsburg had beautiful old trees. What a shame to lose all that."

"Do you have any pictures of downtown?"

"Lots." She flipped several pages. "Here's Main Street from the bridge. And here are all the shops. Oh, look at that. I'd forgotten Marilou's Fabric Shop. Just a little hole in the wall, but she had all the most wonderful patterns, and thread to match all the fabrics. And if you couldn't put a zipper in, she'd do it for you for practically nothing. I wonder what happened to her."

"Wasn't she on your Christmas card list?"

"Yes, she was, but she and her husband moved to Florida, and we lost touch after a few years. Anyway, she isn't your mysterious body. I'm sure Marilou was forty or more when I knew her."

I turned the pages quietly for a while. The church was there, and the rectory beside it. There was a little redbrick schoolhouse and a general store with the words POST OFFICE in the window. There were vintage houses of interesting design and old frame houses that looked as though they were on the verge of falling down. There were fields planted with vegetables and even a shot or two of an old farmer plowing with a horse-drawn plow. I had difficulty believing some of the pictures had been taken in the twentieth century.

Then there were people. Several pictures showed Father Hartman shaking hands with parishioners in front of the church. There were women at meetings, men at dinner, young men in football uniforms.

"They didn't have a high school in Studsburg, so all the kids went to the one in Denham. That's where I'm from. Harry and I met in the Denham high school."

"Carol, do you have a list of names and addresses?"

"I even have the original," she said. "But it's all faded. Harry made me a new one. I'll go get it."

She came back quickly with several sheets of paper. The original list was a very faded pink or purple, and the new one looked as though it had been typed.

I looked at the newer version. Many names had handwritten notes beside them: died 3/7/66; moved to St. Andrew's Home; moved in with daughter, see Violet Hawkins.

The Degenkamps, too, had a note beside their name. "Moved in with son, Eric." Eric's address preceded Henry and Ellie's and had been changed twice. It was a very organic list. Hardly any entry remained unchanged from the original.

"I can get you a copy," Carol offered.

"I would appreciate that."

"Harry can do it tomorrow. I'll drop it in your mailbox Friday morning."

I handed the pages back to her. "Carol, you must have been in your twenties the year you lived in Studsburg."

"I was. Just twenty when we were married."

"Did you know most of the girls in Studsburg who were your age?"

"I knew some of them. I had my own friends in Denham, but I knew a few in Studsburg."

"And none of them disappeared after Maddie's christening?"

She shook her head. "I wish I could help you."

"Maybe your husband can. He grew up in Studsburg. He should remember all the girls in town. He said last weekend he knew everyone. Can I call him tonight?"

"Of course you can." She closed the album and took the address lists back. "I'm glad you're looking into this. Burying a body in a church like that is a desecration."

"I'll see what I can do," I said.

7

As it turned out, I didn't have to wait till Friday for the list. Carol Stifler had run out after I left and had it duplicated. That evening she and Harry knocked on my door about eight o'clock, carrying a cake and a fresh copy of the list. I made coffee and we talked.

"Well, you're right," Harry said. "I did know everyone in town, and I remember all the people I grew up with." He took the list he had just brought for me, pulled a pen out of his breast pocket, and slid it down the first column of names. "The Bakers had a girl named Linda. She got married about a year after I did." He pointed to an inserted address. "Linda Eastman was a little older and left Studsburg before I did. Doesn't she live somewhere around here, Carol? I think we ran into her last year."

"New Rochelle," his wife said. "She had an envelope full of pictures of her granddaughter. I thought we'd never get away."

He went down the alphabetical list, accounting for every child of every parent. Even if the coroner's estimate of the victim's age was off by ten years, there was no one in Studsburg who could have been buried in the basement of St. Mary Immaculate.

"So that's it," he said, slipping his pen back into his pocket as he came to the last name on the list, Walter Zanders.

"What about people who worked in Studsburg and lived somewhere else?"

"Like Mrs. Castro in the rectory? There were some like that. Jackie Peters, who helped out in the gas station sometimes. A few boys from the high school used to get summer work with the farm families. Let's see." He looked down at his empty coffee cup for a full minute. "If there was anyone else, it's gone."

There had to be someone else. I asked him about young men who might have had a girlfriend from another town, as he himself had, but that question seemed to press his memory further than he could handle. "It's a long time, Kix. I can remember who they married, but it's a stretch to remember who they went out with. Some of those fellows had a lot of girlfriends."

I thanked them both and saw them to the door. Sitting at the dining room table, I went over the list, marking the names of people who now lived in the Studsburg area or anywhere else that I considered accessible. The Degenkamps were in Ithaca living with their son, who was a professor at the Cornell College of Agriculture. The mayor, Fred Larkin, had first moved near Owego, and then, in the late sixties, moved again, this time to a town I found on my map not far from Studsburg. I wondered why the Stiflers hadn't invited the Larkins to the baptism. Father Hartman was listed, too. After a brief stint of about a year at the chancery in Rochester, he had obviously been assigned a new parish in another small town in the diocese. He would be relatively easy to reach by car or phone if I had any questions.

But the important question, the one that would start me

on my way, was still far from being answered. I did the dishes from our coffee hour, pressing my imagination to come up with something. Then I went upstairs, showered, and got ready for bed. But I sat propped on my bed for a long time, mentally reviewing the photos I had seen that afternoon in the photo album, the questions I had asked the Stiflers. Harry's example of Mrs. Castro, the rectory housekeeper, was exactly the kind of person I was looking for, a woman who came to town in the morning and left in the evening. I knew without asking that Mrs. Castro would be too old to fit the description of the victim. Rectories didn't hire twenty-five-year-old women as housekeepers. But maybe somebody had had a maid.

As the thought hit me, I swung my feet over the edge of the bed and put my slippers on. Then I got up and started walking. There had to have been a couple of rich families in Studsburg, and they would very likely have hired someone to clean and maybe even cook for them. It didn't take a red-hot imagination to figure out the kind of scenario that could lead to murder: a rich young man, a pretty young girl from the wrong kind of family, a love affair, perhaps with the complications that seem almost inevitably to ensue.

I rubbed my hands on my arms to warm myself, having put the heat down for the night when I came upstairs. Suddenly my blood was circulating overtime. The clock on my night table said 10:10. Too late to call the Stiflers. I got back in bed and turned off the light, certain that I had it. Some family in the area had missed their daughter but had not reported it, perhaps because they mistakenly thought she had run away with a forbidden young man. Being a maid, she wouldn't be included in the Stiflers' guest list, *but if she was seen around the church on the Fourth of July, no one would be surprised*. She belonged there even if she didn't really belong.

A little while later, reaching unsuccessfully for sleep, I felt the excitement of the chase translate itself into sexual excitement. I wished Jack were there. Things would be so much simpler—and more gratifying—if we lived together, but we were nowhere near that. He was a confirmed New Yorker, and I was dedicated to life in Oakwood. I stretched and turned. We would work everything out. I was on my way.

Fifteen of my thirty years were spent at St. Stephen's Convent. Having left after much soul-searching and for none of the popular reasons of today—a man or a crisis of faith—I have many friends there. The best of them is the General Superior, Sister Joseph, whom I met the moment I stepped into the Mother House of the convent when my aunt delivered me on what I always think of as the worst night of my life. Joseph is a good fifteen years older than I, which was a great help during my early years at the convent but has never proved a hindrance to our friendship. On Thursday morning I called her.

"Chris, it's good to hear from you. How's the law work going?"

"It's on and off, hectic, and very satisfying. How are you?"

She was fine and had tidbits of news for me, which I listened to eagerly. "But I imagine you have news to tell us," she said finally.

"More like a request." I gave her as brief a description of the Studsburg murder as I could manage and then came to my point. "I think I may be onto a way to identify the victim, but I'll need to question people in the Studsburg area, and I can't drive there every day."

"Of course not. You'll have to stay overnight."

"Which I can't afford."

"But if you had a place to stay, like a convent . . ." She left it hanging tantalizingly.

"It would be wonderful," I said.

"I can't get you into a Franciscan convent; there aren't any in the area. But that won't bother you, will it?"

"Any place that takes me is fine."

"Give me some time to work on it."

Arnold Gold had some work for me, so I took the train into the city and put in several hours. He was defending a homeless man who had been accused of assaulting a tourist, falsely accused as far as Arnold was concerned. As I looked over the documents, I found that I agreed with him.

When I got home, I took a chance and called the sheriff's department upstate to see if there was any news from the dentists.

"Wish I could tell you something," Deputy Drago said. "We did hear from one old fellow who searched his records right away and found nothing. That's about where it is."

I asked him again to keep me in mind and rang off. A little while later, the phone rang.

"Chris," Sister Joseph's voice said, "I've been trying you since early afternoon"

I explained I'd been in the city and asked what was up.

"I got an OK from the first convent I called. It's just over the New York border in Pennsylvania, about twenty or thirty miles from where I estimate your Studsburg to be. How does that sound?"

"It sounds wonderful. What order are they?"

"They're Josephites. It's a small convent, and most of the nuns are older women, but that shouldn't make a difference."

"It doesn't."

"I think they'd be pleased if you participated."

"I look forward to it."

She gave me all the necessary particulars and I wrote them down, feeling a sense of excitement. People who are professional investigators, or professional anythings, have many options and great flexibility compared to an amateur. I can't charge expenses to a client and I am therefore limited by my pocketbook, which is very spare. Having a safe, inexpensive place to stay—I would contribute to the convent—gave me the edge I needed to proceed.

First I called Harry Stifler.

"Yes, you're right," he said in answer to my question.

"There were some families with money, and they did have housekeepers. The Randalls had a woman about the age of my mother, I'd guess, a Mrs. Quinn who'd been there for years. I wouldn't be surprised if she went with them when they moved. But there was a young girl who worked for the Eberlings, and you know, there may have been a little hanky-panky going on. Check that list, Kix. I think they moved not too far from Studsburg."

He mentioned two other families, the Newburys and the Ritters, both of whom had young women in their employ. All three names were on the list, and the Ritters had apparently settled in a town in Westchester County, which is where I live. I got the number from information and called.

"Hello?" an old woman's voice said.

"Mrs. Ritter?"

"Yes? You'll have to speak up, please. I don't hear so well."

"Mrs. Ritter," I said, raising my voice, "I'm a friend of Harry and Carol Stifler, who used to live in Studsburg."

"Studsburg? My, I haven't talked to anyone from Studsburg for a long while."

I gave her a short explanation. "I was wondering about the young lady who worked for you in Studsburg. Do you remember her?"

"You mean Darlene?"

"Yes, it could have been Darlene. Do you remember her last name?"

"Yes, it was Jackson, Darlene Jackson. She used to come and clean for us a couple of times a week. That was a big house we had in those day."

"Do you know what happened to her after you left Studsburg, Mrs. Ritter?"

"She got a job somewhere; I don't remember exactly. I think she may have gone to work for a real estate man or something like that."

"Did you ever hear from her?" I asked.

"Yes, we did. A couple of years later she sent us an invitation to her wedding. We didn't go, of course, but we sent a nice present. I think that's what she wanted. And then a year or so after that, we got a snapshot of her with a little baby, and we sent another present. I don't think we heard from her after that. The little fellow must be nearly thirty now.''

I had cringed at her interpretation of why the wedding invitation had been sent. ''I expect so,'' I said, crossing her name off my list of possible leads.

When I'd hung up, I checked the address for the Newburys. They had moved to Florida, and I decided to wait before calling them. Instead, I called Father Hartman.

''Yes, Chris,'' he said when I reminded him who I was. ''Good to hear from you.''

I told him I was informally looking into the Studsburg murder, and he asked if anything new had come to light.

''The coroner determined the victim was a young woman—I suppose you know that.''

''Yes, I heard something on the news.''

''And the sheriff's department is trying to find out who she is by looking for old dental records. So far, they have only one dentist who's checked, and he can't find a match. I'm afraid if we wait for the law enforcement people to move, another thirty years may go by, so I'm going to look into it myself.''

''Well, I wouldn't be surprised if an amateur does better than the professionals. Do you have any idea who she was?''

''I think she may have been someone who didn't live in Studsburg but who worked there, like a housekeeper. I wondered if you remembered any families that had young women working for them.''

''Interesting idea,'' he said. ''And there were people like that. The ones I think of first off were the Ritters. They were members of the church and they had a girl who came in to work for them a few times a week. I don't remember her name.''

"It was Darlene Jackson," I said, and explained how I knew. "Can you think of anyone else?"

"Well, let me explain something first about Studsburg. It was not a monolithic town. I'd say it was fairly evenly divided between Catholics and Protestants, although St. Mary Immaculate was the only church in town. And there were a few Jewish families as well. Except for the usual neighborly squabbles, I'd say it was a model community. But as a pastor, I knew my parishioners well, and the other townspeople much less well. There were many families I never met, so I'm probably not your best source."

"Did you now the Eberlings?" I asked.

"Everyone knew them," he said. "They had a very big house and a lot of money. Their church was in another town. J.J. published the local newspaper, and I used to see him when I went down to put in a church notice. I don't think I ever met his family. You want to know if a young woman worked for them?"

"Yes."

There was a silence. Then he said, "There was some gossip, Chris. It's a long time ago, and I've never thought much of gossip. I'd feel better if you didn't ask me about it."

"Sure," I said. "Aside from the Eberlings and the Ritters, were there any others?"

"There must have been, but I really don't remember. I know I'm not being very helpful."

"But you have been, and I appreciate it. Will it trouble you if I call again?"

"Not at all, Chris," he said, sounding genuinely sincere. "I know I balked on the Eberlings, and I have no doubt someone will fill you in on the reason, but I want to know who that poor person buried in my church was as much as you do, and I'll do whatever I can to help."

As I sat down with the paper a few minutes later, I remembered the brief exchange between the Degenkamps the afternoon we met before the baptism. Something about scandals and a sharp caution from Ellie. Henry had eased out of it smoothly with an innocuous tale of embezzlement. Had that been a quick substitution for the Eberling scandal? I couldn't be sure, but I knew what my first destination would be after I returned to the old town.

I put in a full day at Arnold's office on Friday, taking only a few minutes off to call the convent and confirm our arrangement. I had decided to drive up on Sunday, stay over one night, and return on Monday. My class was Tuesday morning, and I could decide then whether to return. The nun who answered knew who I was and said any time I arrived would be all right, and if I happened to come during evening prayers—

"I'll wait in the chapel," I said.

"We look forward to your visit, Christine."

During the afternoon I took some papers into Arnold's office, and he invited me to sit down. "I hear you may not be available next week," he opened.

So I told him about Studsburg. Give Arnold an entrée into a legal case and he's all ears. "Thirty years dead and buried," he said reflectively. "Before I got to know you, I wouldn't have given you a chance in hell of finding anything useful, but I guess if anyone can, it's you." He was referring to the first case I'd fallen into, when I'd met him. "Certainly smacks of premeditation. And you've pretty much accounted for all the young girls in town?"

"If my sources are right, and I have no reason to think they aren't."

"I like your idea that it was someone who came and went. Of course, it may have been someone from far away who was inveigled there just to meet her death. If that's so, the dentists won't turn up anything, and you've got lots of problems."

"I'll let you know after I've given this a try."

"You have someone to stay with up there?"

"I'm going to a convent in northern Pennsylvania."

He gave me a strange look. "You aren't thinking of going back, are you? We really need you in this world."

As tough and ornery as he is, Arnold is the sweetest man I know. He's become something of a father figure to me, and I sometimes think he thinks of me as his youngest daughter. "I'm here to stay," I assured him.

"You need me," he said, "you call collect."

8

Jack came up on Saturday afternoon, and we fulfilled a fantasy of mine by turning our kiss at the door into an act of love in very little longer than it takes to say it. Later on we went down to the private beach on the Long Island Sound that I have a part ownership in, and we walked on the sand. It was cold and windy, and I remembered the first time we had walked here during the summer, when we had just met and I was just getting used to being Christine Bennett and not Sister Edward Frances. This time we walked holding each other, partly for warmth and partly for all those other reasons lovers have for staying close. It was a placid, comfortable afternoon, finishing with dinner out. Jack stayed over, keeping my bed warm and my excitement high.

In the morning we were both up early, and after a good breakfast, he left for Brooklyn and I set out for a convent in Pennsylvania and the beginning of a great adventure.

There is a certain feel to a convent. When I was thirteen it was seductive, beckoning to me. When I was thirty and knew I was soon to leave, it was like a mother's open arms, there when I needed them but not stifling. They could not hold me anymore, but they would never reject me.

I arrived at the Convent of the Sacred Heart at three in the afternoon and was greeted by Sister Gracia. As Sisters of St. Joseph, they were dedicated to teaching, and ran a school for the lower grades on the convent property. Although wearing the habit had become optional, all the nuns I saw had adopted black suits with skirts at midcalf and a modified veil that exposed some hair above the forehead. The voluminous habit of decades ago was now part of their history. That afternoon most of the nuns were out walking or visiting. A few were in their "store" selling the nuns' "products," homemade preserves for which they were well known. There were no postulants or novices this year; it was an aging convent that would not endure much beyond the start of the twenty-first century.

Sister Gracia showed me to my room, a small, spare dormitory-style room with one window, a small closet, and the essential furniture in worn, but well cared for maple. Like all rooms in a convent, this one had no mirror.

First I made my bed with the sheets I had brought. I also had my own towel and soap, and when the bed was made, I found the communal bathroom down the hall and washed, brushing and pushing my hair into a semblance of shape by feel. Although it had grown a couple of inches since I had left St. Stephen's, it still lacked a definite style. Style would come with time. I had found love and work and satisfaction in the months since I had taken up residence in Oakwood. I could live with unstyled hair.

When I had hung up my clothes, I went downstairs and offered myself at the kitchen. A nun in her mid-sixties turned away from the sink and smiled at me.

"You must be Christine Bennett. I'm Sister Concepta. You don't have to do a thing, but if you want to, there are potatoes and carrots to peel."

I sat at an old butcher block and worked, perversely enjoying the opportunity to do on a large scale what I disliked doing at home on a very small scale. Sister Concepta seemed happy to have company. We talked about the convent and then about the Studsburg murder. The nuns had visited St. Mary Immaculate a few weeks ago when the county engineer had proclaimed it safe. They had gone in a bus and prayed inside. No one, of course, had imagined what lay buried in the basement.

Together we cooked the nuns' dinner.

"We have some wonderful grapefruits a friend sent up from Florida," she said. "And for dessert, some lovely ice cream. I hope you like vanilla fudge."

"I like everything," I said.

When the meat and vegetables were cooking and the tables set, Sister Concepta took me for a walk around the convent grounds. There were a couple of acres of farmland now planted with winter rye. The nuns prided themselves on being self-sufficient when it came to vegetables and berries. She showed me a small orchard of old apple trees, the blueberry bushes, the strawberry field covered with salt hay for the winter, and the raspberry canes. We looked in at the store, and I admired the hand-labeled jars arranged neatly on shelves. Finally we went together to evening prayers.

Although I had not left St. Stephen's because of matters of faith, my faith was presently undergoing some questioning and some revision. Without consciously making a decision, I had stopped attending mass on a regular basis during the summer. And since the first time Jack and I had made love several weeks ago, I had not gone to confession. As each week passed, I became more confused about my need to confess what was clearly a sin in the eyes of the church, while, at the same time, I became more comfortable with my physical desires and my physical and emotional relationship with Jack. I knew that sex didn't automatically mean we were destined for a lifetime relationship, but on the other hand, it meant, for me, a wholly exclusive relationship for as long as it lasted, and I hoped—I believed—that Jack felt the same.

As I entered a pew in the rear of the chapel, in this place that reminded me in spirit of the convent that I had loved so much and for so long, I felt a hope that I could reconcile both parts of my life. As I joined the nuns singing "Here I Am, Lord," I experienced a closeness to my religious past that I had not felt in any of the churches I had attended since leaving St. Stephen's.

I spent a very enjoyable dinner and evening with the nuns, who kindly asked me nothing about my life as a sister, and instead, perhaps because they were more interested, talked about the body buried in St. Mary Immaculate. They also routed me to the town where the Eberlings lived and agreed with Joseph's estimate that it was no more than thirty miles from the convent to Studsburg.

I joined the nuns for morning prayers at five-thirty and then for breakfast. It was too early to leave, so I helped clean up the breakfast dishes and do some housework. At nine I got in the car and started off.

It wasn't hard to find. The Eberlings had exchanged a big old Victorian for a modern, architect-designed home of the early sixties. Somehow I expect large, expensive houses to be in wealthy suburbs of big cities, but that isn't always true. There were several houses of the same stature along the road, many with walls, gatehouses, and long private roads to compounds invisible from the road. The Eberlings' house was one of those, although there was no gatehouse and I turned in to the drive without a security check. I had intentionally not announced my arrival to make sure the family would not dream up a reason not to be home.

The door was opened by a woman in a maid's uniform.

"I'd like to see Mr. or Mrs. Eberling," I said.

"And you are . . . ?"

"Christine Bennett."

That was apparently enough, because she asked me to wait, and left. She returned a few minutes later and asked me to follow her.

"Do I know you?" a handsome woman about seventy asked as I entered a beautiful little sitting room.

"You don't, Mrs. Eberling. I got your name from some people who used to live in Studsburg."

"Studsburg!" She smiled, sounding surprised. "Come in, dear. What was your name?"

"Christine Bennett. Chris." I walked over to the sofa where she was sitting and offered my hand.

"Annie, take Miss Bennett's coat, will you?"

I took it off and sat in a chair. Mrs. Eberling called for coffee, and Annie left with my coat.

"Who were the people you mentioned?"

"The Stiflers."

"Stifler? I don't remember anyone named Stifler. You're sure they lived in Studsburg?"

"Their infant daughter was baptized on the Fourth of July thirty years ago, the day before the town was closed."

"Yes, I did hear about that, but we weren't invited. We were gone by then, of course. We commissioned this house a few months after the decision was made to flood the town, and we moved in a good month before the end. We came back that last evening for the fireworks, though. A lot of people who'd moved away did. And of course, J.J.—that's my husband—kept the paper up till the end."

"You mean the press was still operating the day the town closed?"

"Well, no. The businesses all had to close before that. The people who lived there were supposed to be out, too, but that girl was pregnant and the army let her stay till she gave birth. And then there was the christening, and everyone seemed to want to celebrate the Fourth one last time in Studsburg. We always made a big fuss about the holiday."

"How did your husband publish if the press was closed?"

"Oh, he made some arrangement with another paper, I think. It was foolish of him and cost a lot of money, but he said he felt like the captain of a ship, and his paper would come out till the last day."

"So he came back to Studsburg to gather news every day?"

"It was only a Tuesday and Friday paper, but yes, I suppose he did. Though now I think of it, I wonder where he worked from." She looked thoughtful. "I think the priest may have given him a room in the rectory. That was one of the last buildings to go, you know."

"Yes, I heard."

"And would you mind telling me what your interest in all this is?"

"A body was found in the basement of the church in Studsburg last weekend," I said.

"So I heard. Wasn't that simply awful? Do they know who she was yet?"

"Not yet, no. I'm working on behalf of an interested party who's trying to find out." I neglected to say that I was the interested party.

"You mean you're a private detective?"

"No, I'm not, Mrs. Eberling. I've just had some experience in investigating." It's amazing how truthful you can be when you're trying to avoid telling the truth.

"And how did you think I might help you?"

"Well, we're pretty sure that the woman isn't anyone who lived in Studsburg, so we're checking out people who worked in town but lived elsewhere. I understand you had a young woman as a housekeeper. I wonder if you could tell me about her."

"Don't answer that, Mother," a woman's voice said somewhere behind me.

I turned and saw an attractive woman, probably in her forties, coming into the room.

"You really don't want to dredge all that misery up again," Mrs. Eberling said.

"Keep quiet, Mother." The woman turned to me. "Who exactly are you and what do you want here?"

"She knows people in Studsburg, Alicia," Mrs. Eberling said. "It's about that body they found in the Catholic church."

"Well, let the Catholic church worry about it. It's no business of ours."

"I'm just asking for information," I said as pleasantly as I could manage. "The Ritters were very cooperative when I called. They had a girl who worked for them, too."

The daughter laughed harshly. "That stupid little Darlene. I remember her. She worked for us before she went to the Ritters."

"Oh yes, I remember Darlene," Mrs. Eberling said. "Rather a nice girl, except . . ." She trailed off.

"I was interested in the person who worked for you after Darlene left," I said, beginning to understand the chronology.

"I think it's time for you to leave," the daughter said.

"Mrs. Eberling—"

"I think my daughter's right, Miss Bennett. It was a long time ago, and my memory isn't as sharp as it used to be."

"Do you think I could talk to your husband?" I asked without much hope.

"J.J. died," she said with a little smile.

And all the secrets with him, I thought. I got up, thanked her, and went back to the foyer, closely accompanied by the daughter.

"Leave my mother alone," she said in a low voice. "I was only a teenager back in Studsburg, but I know that girl caused my family a lot of grief. We don't need it raked up again. My parents were prominent citizens of Studsburg, and my father left a legacy that few men leave, a record of that town for almost twenty years."

"What did your father do to make a living?" I asked. "I'm sure that newspaper didn't do it."

"My father didn't have to make a living. It had been made for him a long time before. The *Herald* was a gift of love. It never once broke even, but it didn't matter to him. That's how people will remember him, as a generous benefactor. Is that understood?"

I said it was. "Where would I be able to find the *Herald*?" I asked.

"The library in Corning has the whole collection, but you'll have to look at them on microfilm. They won't let anyone but scholars touch the originals."

That was good news, because Corning was on my way home.

"They're all there," she said, "right down to the last day. My father drove to Studsburg and handed them out to people as they were leaving. It was a commemorative issue, with photographs from the nineteenth century right through to the Fourth of July fireworks and the party they had that last afternoon."

"The baptism," I said.

"Yes, that's what it was. It was a wonderful thing for him to do."

"Thank you, Mrs. . . ."

"Whitney," she said shortly.

"Thank you, Mrs. Whitney." I buttoned my coat and went out to my car.

The first thing I did when I left was to find a bank and get some change and then find a pay phone. I am the last American without a credit card. Since I have virtually no financial history, and my own job pays very little, I have a long way to go to qualify for credit. So I pay as I go, and that means using lots of coins when I make a long-distance call from a pay phone. The person I called was Carol Stifler, and she was home.

"I'm upstate," I told her, "and I want to find someone you may have known. Harry said the Ritters had a young housekeeper that last year in Studsburg. Her name was Darlene Jackson. Do you remember her?"

"She went to my high school. I didn't know she worked for anyone in Studsburg."

"Do you know her married name by any chance?" I asked with two fingers literally crossed.

"Uh, let's see." She made little thinking noises while I

waited. "I know someone I can call, Kix. Where can I reach you?"

I explained why I wasn't easily reachable and said I'd call back when I had a chance. Then I drove to Corning.

The librarian was very pleasant and very helpful. She set me up at a microfilm desk and gave me the last microfilm of the *Studsburg Herald*. It started with January 1 of that year. There was very little advertising—not surprising since the population of the town was diminishing each week—but there were several notices of where businesses had moved. I noticed one from Betty's Coffee Shop, which was relocating to Hornell. There were others for shops I had seen in Carol Stifler's album.

I moved the film along. There were no births, no deaths, no meetings, but there were numerous letters from old residents who had made new homes in many different areas. And there was an editorial by J.J. Eberling. It talked about old people making new lives and young people building on strong foundations. J.J. must have had a good time using his paper as a personal forum.

With some anticipation, I turned to what should have been the last edition of the *Studsburg Herald*, and found the film blank. I wound the film along, but there was nothing else on it. Confused, I pressed the Fast Forward key and scooted to the end. There was no commemorative issue, no last photographs, no gift to the people of Studsburg.

I rewound the tape and asked the librarian. She knew nothing. I asked if I could see the original papers, explaining that there was a possibility that the last issue had somehow not been microfilmed. She went to ask someone else, and there was a hushed conversation. Finally another librarian took me downstairs and hauled out the container with the last group of *Herald*s. I kept my hands to myself as she turned to the last copy. It was the last copy on the film. There were no more.

I thanked her for her trouble and went out to my car. The Whitney woman had been detailed in her description of the commemorative issue of the paper. It had to have existed. Had J.J. Eberling changed his mind at the last minute and forgotten to include it with the rest of the collection when he donated it to the library? Not likely for a man concerned about his legacy.

I found a coffee shop and went in for lunch. There was something going on here, although whether it was connected to the body in the basement of St. Mary Immaculate, I could not tell. When I paid my bill I got four quarters in change and found a pay phone. Carol Stifler was home and waiting for my call.

She had spoken to an old friend from Denham and she had everything written down. Darlene Jackson had married Bradley Moore, who was now working for a company in Elmira. The Moores lived just outside the city, and Elmira was on my way home. It didn't take long to get there.

9

Darlene Moore lived in a small, one-story house with a carport instead of a garage. It needed a paint job, but the lawn looked well cared for even it it wasn't green. I rang the bell and heard a response almost immediately. The door was opened by a thin, graying woman wearing dark pants and a sweater. When I mentioned Studsburg, she frowned but opened the door wider. I took it to be an invitation and stepped inside.

"Have you been back?" I asked when we were in the small living room.

"No, but a neighbor of mine drove over to look at the old church."

"I went to a baptism there last Sunday."

"When they found the body?"

"Yes."

"Do they know who it was?"

"No one seems to have any idea."

"Well, I sure don't know." She laughed.

"I spoke to Mrs. Ritter the other day," I said.

"Oh, Mrs. Ritter, yeah." She nodded her head. "How is she?"

"She sounds good. I understand you worked for her for a while."

"I did, yeah. It was a long time ago. Before I got married."

"Did you work for the Eberlings before that?"

"Yeah, sure. The Eberlings. They still alive?"

"Mr. Eberling passed away," I said, using the euphemism for her sake, not my own.

"Well. That's interesting," she said. She gave me another quick, nervous smile.

"Do you know who went to work for them when you left?" I asked.

"Oh, I know," she said.

"What was her name?"

"I don't understand why you want to know all this stuff."

"It's really a long shot," I said, trying to sound very casual, "but I think there might be a connection between the young woman who worked for the Eberlings and the body in the Studsburg church."

"You think he killed her?" She stared at me with a face full of fear and surprise.

"I don't know what happened," I said. "But if you could tell me her name." I met her eyes.

"It was Joanne," she said, her face still pinched. "Joanne Beadles. We went to the same high school."

"Did she stay on with the Eberlings after they moved?" I asked.

"I don't know what happened to her."

"You mean she left the area?"

"I don't know. I just never saw her again."

"When was the last time you saw her?"

"It was so long ago," she said. "I just don't remember that well."

"Were you friends?"

"Yeah, we were friends."

"Did you ever call her after she stopped working in Studsburg?"

"I suppose I could've. I just don't remember."

"I want to ask you kind of a funny question, Mrs. Moore. Was there a dentist you all went to? Someone in town that everyone went to?"

"I went to Dr. Sorenson. A lot of people went to him. I wish I'd gone more." She laughed. "When you're young you don't listen like you should."

"Do you think Joanne went to him, too?"

"I couldn't be sure, but yeah, I guess so. What's a dentist got to do with this?"

"They're trying to identify the body they found in the church through dental records."

"And you think it's Joanne?" She looked horrified.

"I think it may be someone who worked in Studsburg but didn't live there. Were you at the fireworks on that last Fourth of July?"

"You mean that big party they had? I wasn't invited. The Ritters had left already and I got myself another job. I didn't know anyone else in town and I didn't live there."

"Mrs. Moore, why did you leave the Eberlings?"

"Don't make me talk about that," she said, shaking her head.

"Did something happen?"

She nodded.

"Did they accuse you of something?"

"Accuse me? It was him that did it."

"Did what, Mrs. Moore?" I asked quietly.

"What do you think he did? What do old, rich men do with young girls?" She covered her face, and I saw her thin shoulders quiver. "Whatever you're thinking, that's what he did. And he did it more than once. I was a scared dumb kid who needed a job. I was afraid to stay and afraid to leave. If I left, I had to tell my mother why, and I was afraid she'd do something awful. And if I stayed . . ."

She didn't have to finish the sentence. "I'm so sorry," I said. "How did you manage to leave?"

"I saw an ad in the paper that the Ritters wanted help, and I got the job. I told my mother it was a smaller house, so it wouldn't be as much work. But with Mr. Eberling, I never been so scared in my life, not once since that happened. I don't think I ever even talked about it till right now."

"Did he threaten you?" I asked.

"You bet he did. And I believed him."

"What did he say?"

"He said if I told, he'd kill me."

It was dinnertime when I got home, and I heated up some leftovers and ate before doing anything else. Darlene Moore had given me the address of Dr. Sorenson as well as she could remember it. She didn't know Joanne Beadles's mother's first name, and there had been no father that she knew of. But she remembered roughly where they had lived.

After I ate, I called Deputy Drago. When he recognized my voice, he said there was no news.

"I have a suggestion," I said. "A girl who worked in Studsburg seems to have disappeared during that last year. It's possible she went to a dentist named Sorenson." I gave him the approximate address.

"No one by that name on my list, but I'll see if his records were given to someone in practice now. Would you mind telling me how you came by this information?"

"I know some people who lived in the town, and I just

got them to go back in their memories. I hope this is your victim."

"Well, so do I. We really don't have much else to go on. The victim didn't have any broken bones we could match up, and nothing else to distinguish her. I appreciate your call, Miss Bennett."

I decided that was one step up from being a pest.

"You're sure this guy Eberling's dead," Jack said when I told him the story later that night.

"As sure as I can be. His wife told me he was."

"Because while the statute has run out on the assault or rape or whatever it was, he could still be tried for murder."

"Well, I'm not going to sit in some musty office looking through death certificates," I said.

"Would you mind if I ran a check?"

"No, of course not." In fact, it made me breathe a little easier.

"So what's the plan? You wrapping it up now?"

"Not till I hear from the deputy. And as a matter of curiosity, I really want to find out what happened to that missing copy of the *Herald*. I talked to Carol Stifler when I came home, and she's pretty sure she remembers J.J. Eberling handing them out at the bridge on Main Street. She said he was just standing there like a newsboy, flagging down the cars as they left town and giving them out."

"Does she have her copy?"

I laughed. "I think she's taking her attic apart tonight."

"You may not be the most popular person in Westchester after this, kid."

"Maybe I'll be appreciated upstate."

"And in Brooklyn. I miss you."

"Me, too."

"You going back upstate?"

"Not tomorrow. I'm giving a quiz, and I want to get it corrected before I take off again."

"How was the convent?"

"Very nice. Safe and secure and peaceful."

"Don't scare me."

"But it was good to get home."

"You go back to a convent, I ride in on a white horse and rescue you. Don't forget that."

It was a nice image. I promised I wouldn't forget.

My Tuesday morning class is really two class periods back to back. We take a five-minute break at halftime and then continue. When it's over, I feel a little worn-out, but less so on that Tuesday because I'd given them a quiz, which meant I worked less in class and had more ahead of me out of class. I took the papers home and graded them that afternoon. Some of my students had fine critical minds, which I appreciated. Others didn't but tried hard, which I appreciated just as much. This isn't the kind of course anyone fails if they do the assignments.

When I finished with the quizzes, I prepared next week's lesson, leaving me essentially free for the next six days. Then I called Information upstate and asked if there was a Beadles around where Darlene Moore remembered her friend having lived. There wasn't, and even a helpful operator was unable to locate one in the nearby towns.

I wasn't surprised. Thirty years is a healthy generation. A woman who was forty thirty years ago could have died, remarried, or moved several times over. I felt lucky to have located Darlene Moore after so long a time.

Jack called as I was trying to decide what to do next, if anything. "He's dead, OK," he said. "John Jacob Eberling died August seventeenth, 1988. So you won't have to look over your shoulder."

"Thanks, Jack."

"Which means if he's your killer, the case is moot."

"But is it provable?" I said, thinking out loud.

"I don't think you should touch it. There's big money and lots of power there. The cop I talked to knew the name right off. If that daughter of Eberling's wants to fight you, she'll probably succeed."

"She can't stop me from asking questions and reading documents in a library."

"I won't even try to make you change your mind, but do me a favor and be careful."

I promised, hung up, and two minutes later got the call I had been hoping for. Carol Stifler had found the *Herald*.

Harry Stifler walked in while we were looking at the pictures in the thick, yellowing, small-format small-town paper. The entire first half of it was given over to the afternoon and evening festivities—the picnic and the fireworks—and the second half to mainly photographic reminiscences, with an occasional paragraph written by an "old-timer." Interspersed were brief articles telling where the inhabitants of Studsburg had settled or intended to move. Although I was drawn to the second half, I controlled my curiosity and went through the photos of the last day with Carol and then with Harry when he joined us.

Both of them had known Joanne Beadles slightly, but neither knew she had worked for the Eberlings. Since every snapshot had a caption, we went through those first. Joanne Beadles's name was nowhere.

"Maybe she's one of the out-of-focus people in the background," I suggested.

So we went through every picture—there were pages of them—again, looking at out-of-focus faces, not the easiest thing on one's eyes. Carol produced a magnifying glass, which helped a little, but out of focus is out of focus, regardless of the size.

"Maybe I just don't recognize her," Carol said, taking her glasses off and rubbing her eyes. "She was dark, wasn't she, Harry?"

"Dark hair, not too long. But everyone in these pictures has dark hair. Even people I know were blond don't look blond in newsprint."

"Let's eat before it gets cold," Carol said.

We sat down and spent several silent moments, probably all three of us trying to figure out where to go next. Finally I said, "Maybe she's not in a picture. Maybe one of the little articles says something about her."

Since there didn't seem much else to do, we sat and dipped into every boring article—"Luke and Joan Jensen are happily ensconced in their picture-perfect colonial along the shore of Lake Chautauqua. . . . Father Gregory Hartman is looking forward to a year at least at the chancery in Rochester. . . ."—when we'd finished dinner. Dozens of names were mentioned, but Joanne Beadles was not among them.

By that time it was after eight, and I sensed that we all needed a respite from Studsburg.

"I'm going home," I said. "We've worn ourselves out and come up with nothing. Let's just sleep on it."

They assured me they had enjoyed seeing all the old faces again and promised to keep the paper handy. Harry got my coat, and I put it on and got my keys out of my bag.

"Don't you have a pair of gloves, dear?" Carol said. "It's gotten very cold out."

I knew she was right. When I had arrived a couple of hours ago, the temperature had already begun to fall. So I reached into my pocket for the first time since my awful discovery in the basement of St. Mary Immaculate.

10

It was like a replay of that night. As I pulled my glove out of my pocket, something fell with a ping onto the tile floor of the Stiflers' foyer. Carol moved quickly to retrieve it as the sound rang a strong bell in my memory. *I had picked something up off the floor of the church basement as I approached the opening in the wall.*

"Is this yours?" Carol asked, handing me something.

I took it in my hand. "It's from the church," I said, "from St. Mary Immaculate. It was on the floor that night when I found the body."

"You mean the killer dropped it?" Harry said.

"Either that or the body did. The hand was extended toward the opening."

Carol made a face of distaste.

"Well, let's see what it is," Harry said.

The thing was small, thin, oval, slightly dirty, and gold. I rubbed a fleck of caked mud off it. "It's a miraculous medal," I said. Although it couldn't have been more than half an inch long, the engraving on it was a familiar one, the Virgin Mary standing atop a globe representing the world, her foot crushing down a serpent. Medals that size are often family gifts to a newborn, while a larger one might be given to a child at confirmation. Like many Catholics, I wear one myself. "He must have come for it, and when I surprised him, he dropped it and ran."

I turned it over and rubbed the underside. "There's something here. Initials, I think." I moved closer to the light. " 'A.M.,' " I read.

"I'll get the list." Carol dashed away.

"There's a date, too, I think. It looks like . . ." I shook my head. "I don't believe this. The numbers are eight, twelve, ninety-eight. It must mean 1898. That's more than ninety years ago."

"So it couldn't have belonged to the dead girl."

"But she could have ripped it off her killer, and he may not have discovered it was missing until the next day, when it was too late to go back for it."

"Here's the list," Carol said. "Take your coat off, Kix.

I'm not letting you go till we figure out whose medal that is.''

I tossed my coat on a chair and sat down beside Carol.

"Here are the M's," she said, pointing to the first one on her list, Carl Marsden. In parentheses next to his name was the name of his wife, Marian. She moved her finger down the column. All the men's names were later in the alphabet than C, and none of their wives' names began with A. We checked the children's names, which were also listed, and found an Amy Mulholland.

"Do you remember her, Harry?" Carol asked. "It could have been her grandmother's medal."

"The Mulholland kids were young. I don't think she was more than ten or twelve. How old was that girl in the church supposed to be?"

"Twenties," I said.

"Not a likely match. There's a big difference between a ten-year-old girl and a twenty-five-year-old. That coroner may not be very experienced, but I'd think he could tell ten from twenty."

"Even so," Carol said, "I'm going to call the Mulhollands." She took the list and went into the kitchen. We listened quietly as she deftly made conversation with a woman she hadn't known very well and hadn't seen for three decades, starting with her recent visit to Studsburg and how all those wonderful memories had come back. Harry laughed out loud at one point. But when she started asking about the Mulholland children, it was clear they were alive and well.

"Amy lives in Rochester," she said, returning to the living room, "and teaches kindergarten."

"So we're still sure it wasn't someone who lived in town," I said. "Maybe Joanne Beadles had a grandmother whose initials were A.M. Let's see what the sheriff's office finds out. We've done enough for one day."

I put my coat back on and thanked them for everything. This time I put the medal carefully in my change purse. It was the only piece of solid evidence that anyone was likely to find.

The new piece of evidence had complicated the picture, rather than simplifying it. The miraculous medal could not have been given to the victim either at birth or at any other celebration. Assuming only average competence, the coroner could not have mistaken a twenty-year-old woman for one in her sixties—any more than he could have mistaken the remains of a ten-year-old for those of a twenty-year-old. So the medal was originally owned either by someone in the victim's family or by her killer. Perhaps she had grabbed for him as he attacked her, breaking a chain he wore and clinging to the medal in death.

But that would pretty much rule out J.J. Eberling. First of all, he wasn't Catholic. Secondly, he was dead. True, his daughter could have dug up the body, but having met her, I didn't think she had. But if J.J. Eberling hadn't killed the woman in the church, what was his reason for holding back the last copy of the *Studsburg Herald* in the library's collection? And why had he handed them out that last day and then not given the final issue to the library?

Nothing made sense. All I was sure of was that J.J. Eberling had had more than an eye for the young girls who worked in his home. Darlene Moore's story had been very compelling, and I was sure Joanne Beadles had been subjected to the same abuse as her predecessor. But had the outcome been murder?

As I thought about the case, about the photographs in the album and the newspaper, I began to feel a strange sensation of displacement. When I saw the old pictures, I began to imagine how those young people looked today, and when I met people, like the Eberlings and Darlene Moore, I tried to see them as they had been in the last days of Studsburg. I smoothed out wrinkles and colored gray hair. I wanted to feel them as young people. It was as if they had two separate existences, a now life and a then life, with nothing between but a black lake, and the time between those two lives was exactly the span of my own life, which had been anything but a dark lake.

Lying in bed with a flurry of old snapshots racing through my head, I knew that to make sense of what had happened, to come to some satisfactory and satisfying conclusion to this case, I would somehow have to draw the two lives together and make them one.

I willed myself to sleep longer than usual the next morning. Until I heard about Joanne Beadles's dental X rays, I was at loose ends.

The phone rang at nine, as I was finishing my coffee. I carried the cup to the phone.

"Kix? This is Carol Stifler. Am I too early?" She sounded wide-awake and eager.

"It's never too early."

"Harry called his mother last night. They never got a copy of the last *Herald*."

"Really," I said. I felt a little prickle. "Did they leave town when you did?"

"That's just it, they didn't. They helped us pack that morning and load our car. We had a long drive, and I wanted to get the baby to our new apartment as soon as possible. Harry's parents were just moving a few miles away, and most of the furniture had already been moved. I remember the water and electricity were going to be turned off at noon, no matter what, and Harry's mother wanted to go through the house one more time after we left to make sure she had everything she wanted to take with her. She thinks she left just before noon."

"Maybe J.J. Eberling was gone by then."

"Mom doesn't think so. She told Harry she was sure he'd promised to be on the Main Street bridge till everyone in town was gone. He'd promised a terrific last paper."

"Well, he certainly delivered that," I said.

"She also said there were people standing around the bridge looking for him."

"Then sometime between when he gave you your paper and when your in-laws left Studsburg, he changed his mind about distributing it."

"Isn't that peculiar?" Carol said. "I mean, he must have known what was in it when he sent it to the printer. Unless he looked through those pictures that morning and found something."

"Carol, I really appreciate Harry's calling his mother about this."

"Well, we both think you're more likely to dig up the truth than the sheriff's office."

I agreed, but I wanted to hear from Deputy Drago anyway. Sooner or later it would be evidence like a dental match that would confirm the identity of the body.

While floating in my special limbo, I scrubbed down my house, making up for missing my morning walk. I was just about to take out Aunt Meg's precious china from the china cabinet to wash it when the phone rang.

"Miss Bennett, this is Deputy Drago. I've got some news for you."

"Yes, go on."

"We found Dr. Sorenson's files in another dentist's office. Dr. Sorenson retired about fifteen years ago, and he went back through the files himself. Joanne Beadles was one of his patients, just as you surmised. But her X rays absolutely rule out her being that body."

"I see."

"And it looks like we've heard from all the dentists in the area, and they're all a negative. So as far as we're concerned, she's still a Jane Doe."

"Is that the end of your search?" I asked.

"We'll look in a wider circle for a dentist, but frankly, if that woman lived in or around Studsburg, it stands to reason she went to someone around here. People don't drive a hundred miles to have a tooth filled."

"And if she came from somewhere else?"

"Then we've got the whole country to consider, and that's kind of much. By the way, since you mentioned the Beadles woman, I took the liberty of looking her up in the old files. She was never reported missing that I can find."

"I guess I got some bad information," I apologized.

"Hey, I'm glad you cared enough to come forward," he said. "And if you hear anything else, you know where to find me."

I was somewhat cheered by his turnaround; at least if I reached a point where I needed help, he might give it. But the dentists had confirmed my suspicion that not only was the body not that of a Studsburger, it might belong to someone who was only passing through the area. And Carol Stifler's call had reinforced my feeling that J.J. Eberling was somehow involved in the murder. Which left me knowing a few facts but still pretty much in the dark.

I knew I owed Darlene Moore a call to tell her the body wasn't Joanne Beadles. She was home, and she listened with little comment to my brief explanation.

I asked her a few more questions, but she didn't add much to what she had told me during my visit. She had gotten her job through the high school placement office, and she didn't know who had had the job before her. As for Joanne, Darlene had told her why she was quitting, but Joanne had laughed and said she could handle anything.

What I was left with was more of a mystery than I had started with, and also a problem. I had unintentionally picked up a piece of hard evidence, and I knew it was my duty to turn it over to the sheriff's office, but something in me rebelled. With all the fanfare, neither the sheriff nor the coroner had turned up anything except the bullet and the clothes on the body. If I gave the sheriff the miraculous medal, he'd probably make a media event out of it. It would make him look good when he'd done nothing to deserve it, and it probably wouldn't advance the case.

Instead, I called Arnold Gold.

"You turn something up?" he said when he came on.

I told him briefly what had happened and then explained about the medal. "Am I obliged to turn it over to the sheriff?" I asked.

"I get the feeling you're asking the wrong question. Let's talk about a hypothetical situation. Someone picks up something at a crime scene and puts it away and forgets it. Is that about it?"

"That's it exactly. Hypothetically," I added.

"It's not unreasonable for a person to put something in a pocket and forget it for months. Didn't you ever stuff a couple of dollars in a pocket at a toll booth and put the coat away till fall? Happens to me all the time."

I smiled at Arnold's reasoning. Strange as it may seem, it was very unlikely to happen to me, because I am so used to walking around with almost no money in my wallet after years of leaving the convent with fifty cents in my pocket. If I were missing a couple of dollars, I'd know right away. "It sounds possible," I said hesitantly to allow his reasoning to continue.

"Why would this hypothetical person not want to turn this evidence over to the law enforcement people?"

"Because they're dragging their feet, Arnold. Because I know more than they do at this point. Unfortunately, what I know doesn't come together."

"Nothing comes together till the last paragraph, Chrissie," Arnold said in what I had come to recognize as his style. "And since you know my general opinion of law enforcers, I'd say the longer that hypothetical piece of evidence stays lost, the better off it is. As long as I don't need it to defend a client."

"I promise you don't."

"So where do you go from here?"

"With J.J. Eberling dead and no hot prospect for an X ray match with anyone living in town, I think I ought to talk to someone who was likely to know most of the people who worked in Studsburg even if they didn't live there."

"And who's that?"

"The mayor," I said.

"Go to it, girl."

11

I was on the road early Thursday morning, passing signs for towns with names like Roscoe and Deposit and my own favorite, Fishs Eddy. By ten o'clock I was already approaching Binghamton. Getting an early start had not been difficult; what had been tough was telling Jack I might not be back for the weekend.

At Binghamton there are several options open to the driver. You can swing north toward Syracuse and the thruway or continue west along 17 toward Elmira, which was my intended route. Or, I discovered, I could do neither and head northwest toward Ithaca. Ithaca was where the Degenkamps lived, according to Carol Stifler's list, and with a sudden change of direction, I opted for that. An hour later I was just outside the Cornell campus.

A phone book in a coffee shop confirmed the address I had for Eric Degenkamp, and a helpful cashier gave me directions to the house. The streets in Cayuga Heights were winding and beautiful, the houses brick and stone, the lawns and trees showpieces. I parked at the curb in front of the Degenkamp house and walked up a slate path to the front door.

A woman in her fifties answered my ring. "Hi," she said as though we knew each other.

I introduced myself and said I was looking for Henry or Ellie Degenkamp.

"They're both home. Come along. Better keep your coat on. I think they're on the back porch, and it isn't heated."

They were on the back porch, and the sun was so strong, it made artificial heat unnecessary.

Henry saw me come out and said, "It's the young lady from the Stifler baptism."

The younger Mrs. Degenkamp excused herself after we'd all said hello, and I got down to business. The Degenkamps knew about the body in St. Mary Immaculate and were eager to talk about it. They seemed a little put off when my first question was whether they had received a copy of the last issue of the *Studsburg Herald*.

"Well, I suppose we did," Henry said, his brow furrowing. "We got it every Tuesday and Friday."

"This one had pictures of the picnic and the fireworks and a whole section on the history of the town."

Henry smiled agreeably. "If you say so, then I guess we got it. You didn't come all this way to see it, did you?"

"No, I've already seen it."

"You have?" Ellie said.

"Yes. It's a pretty fat issue. You're both in it, you know."

"Then what's the problem?" Henry said.

"It seems that J.J. Eberling gave it to some people and not to others."

Henry shook his thinly haired old head. "It's too long ago for me to remember a newspaper."

I switched to my other area of interest. "Do you remember any young women in their twenties who worked in Studsburg and didn't live there? Maybe someone who was new to the area?"

They looked at each other as though eye contact would help them remember. "I can't think of a soul," Ellie said.

"Maybe a teller at the bank," I prompted. "Maybe someone who worked in the grocery. Could there have been a secretary in the administration building?"

Ellie laughed out loud. "You make Studsburg sound like New York City. There wasn't any administration building. Fred Larkin worked out of his basement, and I'm sure his wife did his typing, all three sheets of it every year. We were only a town of five hundred before the decision came down, and after that, we were a little less every week. We had volunteers for the fire department, and if we needed a policeman, we'd get one from the next town or the state police, or maybe the sheriff's office would send someone over. We just didn't need outsiders."

"You think that girl they found worked in the bank or the store?" Henry asked.

"I don't know where she worked. I don't know if she worked. All I know is she had something to do with Studsburg, and someone killed her. Can you think of anyone who could help me?"

"It can't have been anyone we knew," Henry said. "And if we didn't know her, nobody else would know her. You couldn't walk down the street that last year without bumping into the whole population. There just weren't that many people left at the end."

"You look unhappy," Ellie said to me.

"I am. I keep thinking it's someone everyone knows and isn't aware of, someone . . . ." I looked at my watch. It was nearly noon, and I didn't want to be invited for lunch. "I'm going to drop in on Mayor Larkin. Maybe he'll remember."

"I don't think Fred'll help you any more 'n us," Ellie said.

I got up and started to say good-bye when something occurred to me. "Did you know J.J. Eberling?" I asked. "I mean more than just to recognize."

"Wasn't a friend," Henry said, "but we knew him. He published that paper you were talking about."

"I wonder where he had it printed after they closed down his press."

"No idea," Ellie said.

"Oh, there was a big printer in the next town, Steuben Printers or something like that," Henry said.

"I don't think Steuben did it, Henry."

"Well, thanks anyway." I shook their hands and left them on the porch.

When you leave the New York metropolitan area, all the radio stations that you're used to gradually fade out until they're inaudible. Except for the fact that it's hard to find news, it isn't much of a loss. By chance I tuned in to a central New York station that played fifties music and found myself getting lost in sentimental ballads. As I picked my way through unfamiliar roads, hoping I was traveling in more or less the right general direction, I sensed the suitability of the old music. I was going back in time again to when all the gray heads had color and all the old bodies had vigor and someone was angry enough to kill a young woman.

Carol Stifler's list indicated that Fred Larkin had moved a couple of times since the end of Studsburg, but he had stayed in western and central New York State. Now he lived on a country road that hadn't been paved for a while in a brick house with an old red barn behind it. I pulled into the long driveway and got out of the car.

As I approached the front door, it opened and a man with a beautiful head of gray hair smiled at me.

"Afternoon," he called.

"Mr. Larkin?"

"The one and only."

"Hi," I said, offering my hand. "I'm Christine Bennett."

"You must be the young lady who's trying to figure out that awful murder."

"How did you know?"

"Sheriff's office came and asked some questions. They mentioned your name."

We walked inside and he took my coat.

"If they've already been here, I guess there's nothing new you can tell me."

"Probably not, but I'll do my best. Can I get you a glass of something?"

"No, thanks."

An attractive woman with salt-and-pepper gray hair and an enviable figure came in the room.

"My wife," Larkin said.

I stood and shook hands with her. "Glad to meet you, Mrs. Larkin."

"I'll just let you two talk," she said. "Call if you want anything, Fred."

The mayor smiled after her affectionately. "Well, let's hear it."

"Do you remember Joanne Beadles?" I asked, pretty certain the sheriff hadn't asked that question.

The name didn't seem to faze him. "I can tell you right off there wasn't a Beadles living in Studsburg, not as long as I lived there. And I lived there forty-four years."

"Joanne worked for J.J. Eberling."

"Ah, J.J." Larkin smiled. "Great man, J.J. He's gone now, you know."

"I heard."

"And this Joanne worked in the newspaper office?"

"She was the Eberlings' housekeeper. She worked in their home."

"Those girls came and went," he said. "I wouldn't have any way of keeping track of them. They didn't go to our school or our church or buy in our stores. I'm afraid I couldn't help you."

"But you knew J.J.," I said.

"Oh, sure. If you lived in Studsburg, you couldn't help knowing him. He was one of our most distinguished citizens. Did a lot for the town. Fine gentleman." He took a pipe off the end table beside him and started filling it slowly from a worn leather pouch.

"Mr. Larkin, I think the person who was buried in the church was someone who didn't live in Studsburg but had some connection to the town or to someone who lived in the town.''

''That's why you asked about Joanne.''

''Yes.''

''Well, as I said—'' he began to puff on the pipe as he held a lighted match over the bowl ''—there were any number of girls and women who held day jobs. I don't have any idea how you could find their names today.''

The aroma of the tobacco reached me as he finished speaking. ''That's nice,'' I said.

''Well, Evvie doesn't like it very much. But since she's not in the room . . .'' He raised his eyebrows elfishly.

''What about other people who worked in Studsburg? I understand there was a Mrs. Castro in the rectory.''

''Yes, there was, and Mrs. Castro was sixty if she was a day.''

I hadn't expected to hear she was otherwise, but I wanted him to know I knew a few things about the town. ''What about the bank or the grocery store?''

''Emily Vandermark was about the only woman I know who worked in the bank, and they shut that down pretty fast when people started moving out. Poor Emily was out of a job, and she left town. She'd worked there a good twenty years.''

''And the grocery?''

''That was the original mom-and-pop establishment. Pete and Grace Gilhooley ran that, with their kids helping out as they got older. That was the post office, too, by the way. And pretty near the civic center, if you know what I mean.''

I could imagine. ''Then you can't think of any young woman who worked in Studsburg and lived somewhere else.''

''Not offhand.''

''Maybe someone who came from somewhere else,'' I suggested. ''Someone who was new in town that last year.''

''Why would anyone come to a town that was being put out of business?'' he asked.

I had no answer. ''Maybe one of the young men in town

had a girlfriend from out of town. She could have come to Studsburg just to see him.''

"And he killed her?"

"Perhaps."

"Hard for me to think of boys and their girlfriends after so long a time."

"Mr. Larkin, did you get the last copy of the *Studsburg Herald* from J.J. Eberling?"

"I'm sure I did."

"The thick one, with all the pictures."

"I must have," he said. "I got the *Herald* every Tuesday and Friday of my life."

"Do you still have it?"

He waved the pipe. "Somewhere," he said. "I don't think I could put my hands on it without a search."

"Do you remember what time you left Studsburg that last day?"

"I was one of the last to go. That was my town, and I felt it my duty to stay till the end. I have to admit, it was a tearful parting."

I was feeling pretty down myself at that point. If I could believe him and Mrs. Eberling, both he and J.J. had stayed till the end. Mrs. Eberling had spoken of her husband as the captain of a ship. In my mythology, ship captains stay till the last man is gone. "I thank you for your help, Mr. Larkin," I said, getting up. "I guess it's a blind alley. I just hate to think of a young woman being buried in potter's field."

"I'm sure that won't happen. I'll ask around and get some contributions to give her a decent burial."

"That's very nice of you. May I send you a check for the fund?"

He patted my shoulder. "Let's wait till the sheriff finishes his investigation. Would you like to see a picture of Studsburg taken from the air?"

"Very much."

He took me to a wood-paneled room with a fireplace. There were sports trophies on the mantel and family pictures on the walls. Frederick Everett Larkin's framed sheepskin hung among them.

"A friend of mine took it from a helicopter that last year. It's as clear as they come. You can see almost every building in town."

The photo was large and mounted over the fireplace. The church dominated the near left center, and I could make out Main Street and the famous bridge. "It's beautiful," I said.

He picked up a pointer and touched the photo. "That's where I lived. And here's J.J.'s house. Big, wasn't it?"

"And handsome."

"Here are all the stores on Main Street—the bank, the general store. Here's the old coffee shop. They made the best pie you ever tasted, and a meat loaf that'd knock your socks off. Here's the one and only gas station in town. That's the playground right here. See the bleachers? J.J. bought 'em for us. We had some great ball games there. Here's Simpson's Farm, this big, open space. You ever taste fresh-picked corn?"

"Once or twice."

"Nothing like it, nothing in the world. Here's the road that came through town, this little ribbon. What a beautiful place that town was. And here's the school I went to and my kids went to, and there's the little grove of pines where I asked my wife to marry me."

"Were you married in St. Mary Immaculate?" I asked.

"You bet."

"Thank you for showing it to me, Mr. Larkin. And for the guided tour."

"My pleasure. The best years of my life were spent in that town. Let me walk you to your car." The nostalgic trip through Studsburg had invigorated him. His voice was strong and he moved with youthful agility.

I stuck my head in the kitchen and said good-bye to Mrs. Larkin. Then I put my coat on and we walked outside.

"Nothing like it," he said. "This is a pretty place we live in now and we have a nice life here, but that town was special. I can't tell you the grief when we heard it was going to be flooded. We fought it, of course, but the little people never win those battles.''

The wind was blowing now. ''Were you at the baptism for the Stiflers' baby on the Fourth of July?'' I asked.

''Wouldn't miss it for the world.''

I had known he was there, because Carol had pointed him out in pictures in her album. ''Were you and your wife both from Studsburg?''

''Met her when I was in the eighth grade.''

My hand was on my car door. ''The school,'' I said. ''Who were the teachers?''

''In my memory there were never a hundred kids in the whole school at one time. What we did was, we had teachers who took several classes. Mrs. McCormick must have taught there forty years. I had her, and my son had her.''

''Did she live in town?''

''No, I believe she drove in from somewhere every day.''

''And who were the others?''

''Mr. Dietrich was the other one. That last year the classes shrank down to almost nothing, but we had to keep him on.''

''And that was it?''

''That was it.'' He held out his hand and we shook.

As I backed out of his drive, he stood watching me, and he waved as I reached the road.

In a little while I was on my way to the convent.

12

I was troubled enough by some of the things Fred Larkin had said to make a small detour and drop into the sheriff's office. Deputy Drago was just putting on his hat to go out, and I reminded him who I was and we shook hands.

"I just talked to Fred Larkin," I said.

"The mayor of the old town?"

"Yes. He said your office had already questioned him."

"I did it myself. We looked up his name in the records, and I drove out last week and saw him."

"Did you mention my name to him?" I asked.

We had been walking out to the parking lot. Now he stopped and looked at me. "Why would I do that?"

"He said someone from the sheriff's office had mentioned my name."

"No, ma'am," he said firmly. "First of all, I don't go telling people I'm questioning police business, and secondly, I can't think of one good reason why I would have done it in this case."

"Thanks, Deputy. That's all I wanted to know."

Which meant the Degenkamps had called Fred Larkin after I left.

The car seemed to have a will of its own. Without thinking about where I was going next, I found myself on the little road that led to Studsburg. There were no cars parked at the edge of town, no people walking the streetless streets, snapping pictures of buildings that had vanished more than a quarter century ago. There was just a windowless church rising from the depths of a lake that had dried up.

I stood at the edge for a while and then scrambled down the slope. The crime scene tapes were gone, and the sign warning me to ENTER AT YOUR OWN RISK was staked near the entrance. I took the dare and entered. It was late enough that the sun was nearly down, and without my flashlight, I would have been in trouble. But the floor, if anything, was cleaner than the last time I'd been there. Perhaps they had swept it up, looking for some clue to the man who had unearthed the body.

I walked to the sanctuary, pleading silently for some insight on where to go from here. If Fred Larkin had seen my name in a newspaper article, he would have used that as a reason for knowing about me. But he made up a lie to explain his slip when he recognized my name. It told me he was nervous. The Degenkamps had warned him that I was on my way. Fred Larkin knew something. Or maybe the Degenkamps did, and didn't want Larkin spilling the beans on them.

I remembered that when I had asked them if they knew any young women in their twenties who had worked in Studsburg, they had looked at each other in a way that I had interpreted as prodding their memories. Now it seemed that what they were doing was warning each other to keep silent. There *was* someone, and both the Degenkamps and the Larkins knew who it was. Which meant I was on the right track if I could just figure out which of my many lines of questions was the right one.

It was getting late, and I wanted to reach the convent in time for dinner. Using my flashlight, I went back to my car and then drove south.

The nuns were just leaving chapel when I got there. I sat at dinner with Sister Concepta, who quickly set an additional place for me. The nuns at the table were full of questions, my investigation having sparked their interest and set them all thinking. As we ate, they speculated on who, how, and why.

"If it was a boyfriend killing his girlfriend," Sister Gracia said, "I think it's a dead end. He'll have covered his tracks, married someone, made a new life. Today he'll be a respected citizen, a good father, someone no one would ever suspect had committed a murder. His friends will probably give him testimonials," she finished wryly.

"Even if you don't find him and bring him to justice," Sister Concepta said, "he may suffer from what he did. He may have a terrible conscience."

Sister Gracia waved away the possibility. "People live with their consciences better than we'd like to think. And guilt rarely leaves a mark that we can see. If it did, the police would have an easier job. Unfortunately, guilt isn't like a scar or a tattoo or a scarlet *A*."

I felt she was right. Without some overt mark, I could not identify the guilty conscience in someone I spoke to. I had already made at least one mistake of judgment, putting the Degenkamps in the safe-and-honest category.

"You're right about the girlfriend," I said. "But it seems to me there has to be more to it than that. The coroner said the woman wasn't pregnant, which is the first thing you think of as a motive, especially thirty years ago. It has to be something else, something these older people are trying to keep from me. What could all of them have had in common?"

"The occult," one of the other nuns said. "A witches' coven. God forbid," she added, crossing herself.

It didn't seem likely. I listened as they let their imaginations take hold. Nothing they proposed really grabbed me. When dinner was over, I helped with the washup and then set the tables for tomorrow's breakfast. It wasn't much, but it gave someone old enough to be my mother the chance to take it easy while I was able to burn off the energy I'd stored while sitting on my duff in the car most of the day.

When I was done, I put my coat on and walked over to the chapel. Usually when I visit a church, I light three can-

dles, for my mother, my father, and my Aunt Margaret. I
hadn't done it for a while, so I did it now, leaving a contri-
bution in the box. Because we were schooled strictly in safety,
I sat in a pew till the candles burned down, which took about
half an hour. While I waited, I drained my mind of everything to do with the Studsburg murder. I thought instead of
Jack, of how happy I was when we were together.

The chapel was old and small, dimly lit and fairly low-
ceilinged. There were two confessionals, one on either side.
A priest probably came once or twice a week to hear the
nuns' confessions. It may seem strange to think of a nun
living in austere circumstances, dedicating herself to her
faith, needing to confess, but nuns are as human as the rest
of us. They have feelings, sometimes strong, angry ones,
just as motorists and politicians do, and sometimes they get
out of hand. And they succumb to temptations that the rest
of the world might find surprising. Once, when I was alone
in Aunt Meg's house, I went to her bedroom, the one I now
sleep in, and looked at my face in the mirror. It had been
years since I had seen that face, and I was overcome with the
desire to know what I looked like. Through all the time I
lived in the convent, I had dutifully shunned reflecting windows and pools of water. Now, purposefully, I inspected the
face that was mine but not mine to see, the arch of the brow,
the length of the lashes, the fullness of the lips. When I
smiled at the reflection with satisfaction, I knew I had sinned
in more ways than one. When I returned to St. Stephen's, I
confessed to the priest who visited us regularly and never
looked at my reflection again until I was living in the house
and had met Jack.

Now I carried a different guilt with me. I was engaging
freely and happily in a physical relationship with a man to
whom I was not married. That half the women in the country
were doing the same thing did not excuse or forgive me, and
I was unable to confess. When you confess, you promise not
to repeat the sinful activity, and I was not ready to do that.
True, little children promise week in and week out not to hit

their little brothers or eat too many cookies or disobey their parents, only to return home to do it all again with relish. But I was no child, and I could not make a promise I knew I would break.

Two of the three candles had burned out. I went over and watched the last one as it flickered to its demise. When it was safely out, I returned to the Mother House.

"Christine," Sister Gracia said as she saw me, "you had a phone call a little while ago. Just a minute and I'll get the message."

The little Post-it said that Sergeant Brooks had called, and I could return the call collect. He must have decided that calling a sergeant would be easier than calling a boyfriend.

"If you want a little privacy," the nun said, "there's a phone in the kitchen."

"Thank you." I went to the darkened kitchen, found the light switch, and put my call through.

"Sure, I'll accept," Jack's voice said after answering on the first ring. "Hi, sweetheart. Get there OK?"

"Got here fine, but I made a bunch of detours along the way."

"I've been thinking about your investigation versus our sex life."

"And what did you come up with?"

"That I don't want us to give up either one. Suppose I meet you Saturday at the motel you went to for the baptism."

"Jack, that would be terrific."

"I'm just full of great ideas. I've just had the most boring day of my entire career, so I put my head to work."

"My day was interesting, but I'm getting pulled in several directions."

"It'll clear up when you get closer to the end. Look, I can leave here by eleven, so I should get there by what? Three, four o'clock?"

"Yes. I'll meet you there. What a neat idea."

"Need anything?"

"Not anymore."

"That's what I like to hear."

As long as I had a telephone handy, I called Harry Stifler's mother. I had met her at Richard's baptism, and I knew she would remember me.

"How nice to hear from you," she said. "I've just been watching the most awful movie on television, and I needed an excuse to get away from it."

"I wanted to ask you about Fred Larkin, Mrs. Stifler."

"Fred? Dearest man in the world. Born and raised in Studsburg, and loved it with every bone in his body."

"Did you know him well?"

"Everyone knew him well. He had a full-time job, you know. Being mayor was only a hobby. But it was the kind of hobby that took every minute of his life. He knew everyone. Every baby that got born got a gift from him. Every couple that got married got something. He attended every funeral, visited every patient in the hospital. There just wasn't ever another person like Fred Larkin."

I was sorry I had called and I was dangerously near laughter. Somehow, I had expected to hear complaints, old grievances, and here I was getting the kind of testimonial usually reserved for a eulogy.

"Did you know his wife?" I ventured.

"Lovely woman. Beautiful. It was such a good town, Chris. There'll never be another one like it."

I gave up. I was obviously asking about a place in heaven, and this old woman wasn't going to go on record as having any objections to the celestial governing body.

When I got off the phone it occurred to me that all the information of substance that I had gotten had come from Darlene Moore, who was the one person I'd talked to who hadn't lived in Studsburg. Maybe if you didn't live there, Fred Larkin didn't owe you anything. And you didn't owe Fred Larkin anything. I decided that the next morning I would try to find Steuben Printers.

13

The noise of the presses was constant and seemed to be located on the other side of the wall of the office.

"Yeah, my father printed that little paper for him at the end." The man whose voice was raised to be heard over the din was Kenneth Parker, and the business was Steuben Press. It was located an even mile from the motel I had stayed in.

"I don't suppose there's any chance I could talk to your father." I didn't think there was. Kenneth Parker looked about fifty.

"You're a few years too late. I'm sorrier than I can tell you. My father was a wonderful man."

I said something appropriate. "I don't suppose you remember J.J. Eberling?" I asked.

"Sure I remember him. We printed that paper—" he looked up at the ceiling "—I'd say damn near six months."

"Must have been expensive for J.J."

"He had no choice. They were closing down the shops in that old town, and they wouldn't let him stay on. That crazy little paper was his life. Besides, the expense didn't bother him."

"I heard he had plenty of money."

"He had enough. His column kept him going."

"His newspaper column?"

"He had a syndicated column, ran in forty or fifty papers around the country, maybe more. Couple of times a week. Folksy stuff. You know, pipe-in-the-mouth scribblings.

'Anywhere, U.S.A.' or 'Little Town, America' or something like that. Oh, yeah, J.J. made a living.''

"I heard he inherited money," I said.

"Probably, but we're not talking oil wells. Maybe enough to keep him off the streets."

His widow certainly wasn't living two steps above the poverty level. "You didn't happen to go to Denham High School, did you?''

"That's the other side of Studsburg."

"Then you wouldn't have known Joanne Beadles."

He measured me with his eyes before answering. "That wouldn't be one of J.J.'s little girls?''

"Was he known for that?''

"There was a rumor once. J.J. kept it out of the papers. That was one thing he knew how to do." Parker laughed. "I couldn't tell you if there was a Joanne involved. I couldn't even tell you what it was all about.''

"Was the rumor around the time that Studsburg was flooded?''

"I'd say so."

"I wish I could find someone to tell me about it." I felt my meaning couldn't have been clearer without drawing a picture, and I'm a terrible artist.

"What's your interest in J.J., Miss . . . ?''

"Chris Bennett."

"Miss Bennett."

"A young woman was murdered and buried in the Studsburg church thirty years ago. I want to find out who she was, and I don't think the sheriff is doing a very enthusiastic investigation.''

"And you think she was one of J.J. Eberling's little girls." He said it as though he'd drawn a conclusion.

"I don't know who she was. I'm looking for a lead, anything I can find. I've talked to several people who used to live in Studsburg, and I have the clear sense that I'm being lied to. Not just about J.J.," I added.

"Let's face it, you're looking for someone who hated him."

"I'm looking for someone who wasn't beholden to him," I said.

That was when he smiled. "I see you've got Studsburg figured out. You're right, you need to talk to someone who didn't live there."

"That's why I'm here."

"Because it's no secret J.J. was good to everyone in that town. Folks needed a little help, he came through. And he gave them something no one else in the world could, a chance to feel famous. There weren't more than five hundred people in that town by the nineteen fifties, and it wasn't hard for him to get every one of them in the paper for one thing or another. You having a party? J.J.'ll print pictures of it. You get the math award? J.J.'ll write you up."

"I think I understand."

"It's easy to look the other way when someone's been good to you. He sure as hell didn't do anything good for us. He was the son of a military man, you know, and he came in here all the time like a general commanding his troops. You would have thought he owned the place. It disrupted our business and got our employees angry. He had no respect for anything except his own work, and he expected people to move over and bow down because he was J.J. Eberling. My father was doing him a big favor—I'm sure we lost money on that job—but you'd've thought it was the other way around. Tell you what. Give me your number and I'll do some calling around."

I wrote down the convent number and my own back in Oakwood.

"You staying with those nuns?" he asked.

"Just while I'm in the area."

"Nice bunch of ladies. My wife buys their jams and jellies every year."

"Where would I find Studsburg's records if I needed them?" I asked.

"Good question. I think I heard someone say they're in the county building. You know where the sheriff's office and the court are?"

"I've been there."

"That's it."

"Thanks, Mr. Parker."

"I'll do my best."

The silence outside his office made me feel almost light-headed. I drove to the motel and had a second breakfast in the coffee shop. Although we'd been talking about J.J. Eberling, I felt certain that the word "beholden" could apply just as well to Mayor Larkin. They were both good men to the people in their town, and I didn't have the time or resources to find the potential one or two people from Studsburg who might have had a gripe against them. I needed to find people who didn't live there but knew the town.

I opened my notebook and turned pages while I sipped coffee. Mrs. Castro, the rectory housekeeper, wasn't likely to be alive. Nor was Mrs. McCormick, who had taught school for forty years. The other teacher was Mr. Dietrich, no first name. Fred Larkin had said Mr. Dietrich stayed on that last year even though enrollment was way down. He hadn't said how old Mr. Dietrich was or how many years he had taught in Studsburg.

I paid my bill and found a phone directory near a bank of coin phones. There were enough Dietrichs listed to make my task embarrassing. The thought of calling half a dozen people and asking for a man whose first name I didn't know—and who might not even be alive—gave me pause.

Then I remembered the name Mulholland. On Tuesday evening Carol Stifler had called someone named Mulholland when we were trying to figure out who the miraculous medal belonged to. Mrs. Mulholland had had a school-age daughter named Amy. The list was in my bag. I gathered together enough quarters for a few minutes conversation, and dialed.

"Hello?" a woman's voice answered.

"Mrs. Mulholland?"

"Yes, it is. Who's this?"

I told her.

"Oh yes," she said. "Carol Stifler called the other night. Wasn't that something about the body?"

"Mrs. Mulholland, the Stiflers said you had a daughter about ten or twelve that last year."

"Yes, Amy was in school then."

"I'm trying to reach a teacher from the Studsburg school. Amy didn't happen to have Mr. Dietrich, did she?" I had decided that a woman was more likely to teach the younger classes, leaving Mr. Dietrich the upper half of the school.

"No, Mr. Dietrich left the year before. He'd been there awhile, and the town—what was left of it—didn't feel they could pay him full salary."

My heart sank. "Then Mrs. McCormick taught the whole school?"

"Oh no. They got a new teacher just for that last year to teach the sixth, seventh, and eighth grades. Amy had her."

My heart had begun to pound. "Do you remember anything about her?" I asked. "Her name? Anything else?"

"Amy would remember her name, I'm sure. All I remember is that she was young, just out of school, I think, so we were able to pay her next to nothing, which was all the town could afford. Kind of a pretty thing. The kids all loved her. I remember she wore blue jeans and sneakers once when she took them on a class trip." She laughed. "Who could forget something like that thirty years ago?"

14

It was one of those moments when you want to grab someone and start dancing. I didn't have a name, a reason, or a whisper of proof, but I was sure I had my victim. Mrs. Mulholland had given me Amy's phone number, which I couldn't call till late afternoon as Amy was teaching, but that didn't stop me. I drove to the county building to find some old records.

The people in the records office weren't exactly delighted to hear my request, but after I filled out a form and waited my turn, a woman took me down to a basement room where old files were kept. The files for most of the towns in the county, she explained, were kept right in each town, but since in this case the town didn't exist anymore, the records had been transferred to the county. She couldn't remember the last time anyone had asked to see these, but she knew where they were kept.

It was dark and empty down there till she turned on some lights, and the air was musty. There were only a handful of boxes for Studsburg, and they were labeled by year. If the number of records was any indication of population, Studsburg had dwindled noticeably in the course of the twentieth century. I had no interest in any but the last year or two, and those files were all in one box.

I looked at headings on folders till I found the files for the last two years. It was all there, ads placed in several newspapers and carbon copies of letters written to a variety of college placement offices explaining the need for a junior

high teacher with a valid New York State license for a period
of one year, not renewable. The town offered a salary of four
thousand dollars plus a few benefits. If the file was complete,
only four people applied. Their letters and resumes testified
to their desire to teach in a small town, their ability to handle
three classes at three different levels, their willingness to
cooperate with the community, and their commitment to
good education. Of course, all of them loved teaching junior
high school students more than any other age level. They
sounded spirited and dedicated, their personalities rising from
the old typewritten pages. I would have hired any one of them
myself.

Only one of the candidates was ever interviewed. (The
town sprang for the round-trip fare.) Her name was Candida
Phillips, and according to her resume, she lived in Pennsylvania and was twenty-three when she applied. She was interviewed by a committee consisting of the mayor, Henry
Degenkamp, Terence Scofield, Irwin Kaufman, and, in what
I decided was a sop to the education profession (but not
necessarily to women), Mrs. Adele McCormick, the only
other teacher. It was obviously a town run by its men.

The reports of the five interviewers were in the file. The
mayor found Miss Phillips to be "pleasant, clean, well-
mannered, appropriately dressed, and having an agreeable
disposition." Mr. Degenkamp also found her looks and
manners acceptable and added that "she has the vigor and
enthusiasm necessary to control the age group." Messrs.
Scofield and Kaufman echoed their colleagues' favorable
opinions in slightly different language, and Mr. Kaufman
mentioned that Miss Phillips, "being young and unattached,
can afford starting salary and will surely have no difficulty
finding employment next year with her additional experience." Mr. Scofield found "Candy to be an exemplary young
woman who seems eager to accept the challenge Studsburg's
junior high will offer her." My eyebrows rose as I read his
opinion.

By far the most interesting report came from Adele Mc-

Cormick, who must have conducted the most searching interview of the lot. She determined Miss Phillips to be "well educated and knowledgeable in both pedagogical theory and relevant subject matter. She is personable and answers difficult questions with a demeanor that belies her age." I made the assumption that the "difficult questions" were asked by the gentlemen, probably out of curiosity and for no reason connected to the job. I certainly knew which of the five I would select for my committee.

The job was apparently offered to Miss Phillips on the spot following a brief huddle out of her earshot, and she accepted as quickly as they made the offer. A copy of the contract was in the folder, signed by Fred Larkin, Mayor. I guessed that in a town of five hundred, the mayor functioned as superintendent of schools and maybe as principal as well.

The minutes of the meeting were taken by Mrs. McCormick, who, as the only woman present, was the obvious choice for recording secretary. I wondered if she had also typed the men's reports.

Miss Phillips was paid twice a month, as was Mrs. McCormick, and the canceled checks were there for me to see. There were deductions for social security, which made me gasp; they had increased more than tenfold in the intervening years. Ditto for the Blue Cross/Blue Shield deductions. I knew what Arnold Gold paid for mine in the present. A pittance was taken off for pension, and I made a note to ask Jack to check with Albany to see if Candida Phillips had contributed after that year. If I was building a case, I wanted a good one.

I lingered over her resume. It was typed on one of those mechanical typewriters that you only see in set pieces nowadays. A single error was erased and typed over. I guessed that Wite-Out was not yet a gleam in its inventor's eye.

She had gotten her bachelor's degree at Penn State a year before applying for the Studsburg job, and spent the academic year as a permanent substitute in a school near home. Included in the resume was her high school and a few summer jobs that indicated a person who enjoyed spending time with children. One summer she had been a camp counselor.

It took some searching to find a piece of information I wanted rather desperately, Candida Phillips's address. Since envelopes weren't included, and her address was not on her canceled checks, I found it only because during the school year she wrote a letter to Terence Scofield to request permission to take her classes on a trip to Watkins Glen. At that point I decided maybe Mr. Scofield was "superintendent" of schools. His response was not in the file, but remembering Mrs. Mulholland's description of the young teacher in jeans, I assumed that was the class trip she had been referring to.

The letter of request was typed in traditional business-letter style, starting with Miss Phillips's home address on the right and concluding with "Very truly yours" at the end. I copied down the address with glee.

There wasn't much else in the file except for two "To Whom It May Concern" letters of recommendation for Candida Phillips. Obviously she would need references from her year in Studsburg for future employers, and there was probably an arrangement with the county office to send copies of these letters on her request.

One letter was written by Scofield, who thought she was a "fine young woman, well liked by students, able to get along with staff." I guessed that meant Mrs. McCormick, although it might have meant with him. The other letter was written by Mayor Fred Larkin, who said she had made Studsburg's last year a productive and memorable one for the junior high school.

J.J. Eberling's name was never mentioned anywhere in the school file.

Considering the fact that Mayor Larkin had interviewed her before hiring her and written her a reference, it seemed hard for me to believe that he had completely forgotten her existence. But he had been quite specific when he told me that even though the classes had become much smaller, they had had to keep Mr. Dietrich that last year. And both he and

Henry Degenkamp had been on the interview committee, so both of them knew when I asked for people who worked in Studsburg and lived elsewhere that Candida Phillips was the kind of person I was looking for. So it was possible that one or both of them had killed her and buried her in the church basement. What made that hypothesis implausible was that Ellie Degenkamp seemed to be in on the deception. It was she who stopped her husband from talking about scandals, she who locked eyes with him when I asked about day workers. It's hard to look at people in their eighties and see them as killers.

As long as I had the records in front of me, I went through other files from that last year. The tax rolls were in one folder, and I went down the alphabetical list, which was somewhat shorter than Carol Stifler's list of addresses. The amounts of the taxes were low enough to be laughable. I guessed you could have bought a house in Studsburg for what I pay in property taxes in Oakwood today. Still, with what they were paying their teachers, you couldn't expect houses to be very expensive or taxes to be high. A quick run-through confirmed that J.J. Eberling's property taxes were the highest in town, which wasn't very surprising. And I was pleased to note that St. Mary Immaculate donated fifty dollars a year to pay for garbage collection "and other sundries."

I found a few other interesting things in the tax file. Luther Simpson was granted a delay in paying his second-quarter taxes. Simpson, I recalled from my visit to Fred Larkin, was the owner of the large farm in Studsburg. It occurred to me that spring is when farmers do their planting, when they have all their big expenses. Perhaps the Simpsons were unable to find the money to pay their taxes in the spring, and they put it off till harvesttime, when they would take in the bulk of their income for the year. I had a sense of the hard times farmers face, especially small ones. Elsewhere on the list were other notations of delays granted. Next to one name someone had written in ink: "Pd. J.J.E." The name was that of a woman. The amount was very small, only forty dollars, but if you're old and poor, that's probably enough to feed you for a month; at least it was at that time. My list from Carol Stifler showed the woman to have died two years later after having moved to an address c/o another name.

There were also several property tax amounts crossed out in ink, with lower numbers substituted. I knew it was possible to argue for reduced taxes, but it seemed strange for people who were on the verge of moving away to go to the trouble.

Probably the reason the list was shorter than my address list was that so many people had already left town. After going through all the names once, I decided the time had come to track down Candida Phillips.

15

The house was still standing, which gave me an additional lift. It was about the size of the one I own, on a nice piece of property with an old car sitting in the driveway. The mailbox at the curb had the name Thurston painted on it. When I rang the bell, a woman in her sixties answered.

I introduced myself, and she acknowledged she was Mrs. Thurston. "I'm trying to track down a young woman who may have roomed here a long time ago." I saw her eyes brighten and her face look expectant. "Her name was Candida Phillips."

"Candy!" she said excitedly. "Come on in. Do you know where Candy is?"

Whoopee! Fireworks went off inside me. "I'm afraid not," I said, trying to keep my own excitement in check.

"She most certainly did live here, and when she left, she promised to keep in touch, but we never heard from her again."

I followed her into a bright, shiny kitchen, and we sat at the table. This was obviously a person who had known and liked Candy Phillips, and I decided to go with my instincts and take her into my confidence.

"Mrs. Thurston, I just learned Candy's name a couple of hours ago, and I'm trying to find out as much as I can about her. The only information I have is that she taught school in Studsburg in the year before the town was flooded and that she lived here sometime during that year—"

"The whole year," she interrupted.

"Then you knew her well."

"Oh yes, real well. We just loved Candy."

"I'm not sure," I said hesitantly, reluctant to burst her balloon, "but I think the body they found in the Studsburg church may have been hers."

"Oh no." She clapped a hand over her mouth and looked at me with frightened eyes. "I knew something was wrong when she didn't come back that last night. Who could ever have wanted to kill Candy?" she said, dropping her hand and reaching for a tissue. "She was the dearest person you can imagine."

"I don't know. But I want to find out."

"Would you mind if I called my daughter?"

"Of course not."

"She knew Candy better than anyone." She dialed a number and, without any introduction, began to explain that a woman was here asking about Candy Phillips. "Well, drop everything," she said. Then she hung up. "It won't take her a minute. Monica waited so long to hear from her. She just couldn't believe Candy would leave and forget us."

As she stopped speaking, I could hear the front door open and a woman's voice called, "Hello? I'm here."

Her name was Monica Anderson, and she was the youngest person I'd met since starting the investigation. She must have been about forty.

"Of course I remember Candy," she said. "She was the brightest light of that awful year. My dad died, and Mom had to rent out a room to make ends meet, and she was sure she was going to get a thief who had loud parties and dropped her clothes all over the house, and then Candy came and she was like a gift to us."

"I really needed the money," Mrs. Thurston said, "but after a few months, I would have let her stay on for nothing just to have her around." She turned to Monica. "This lady thinks Candy may be the body they found in that old church."

"Oh, no, not Candy," the daughter said, her face resembling her mother's as she had heard my suspicion.

"Tell me about her," I said gently.

And prodding each other, reviving each other's memories, they did. Candy had come to them through a realtor with whom they listed the rental room, terrified of putting an ad in the paper, not knowing how to turn down someone they found undesirable, not even sure how to identify such a person. Candy had come with a large, battered suitcase and a bright new train case that had a mirror in the top when you opened it. She had moved into the smallest bedroom in the house sometime before the school year started—"She had a lot of preparation," Mrs. Thurston said—and she just became part of the family.

"Did she have a car?" I asked.

"Oh yes," Monica said. "It was an old Volkswagen with the two little windows in the back. It must have been as old as I was."

"She needed it to get to school every day," Mrs. Thurston said. "And she washed it every Saturday, even in the rain." She laughed, and I felt myself drawn into the circle.

"Would you like to see her room?" Monica asked.

I said I would and we went upstairs. The room still looked as though it was made for a single person. There was a bed, a dresser, a night table, and a scarred old oak desk. It was a corner room, and there was a window on each outside wall. Crisp white curtains hung in two tiers down to the sill.

"It's almost the same as when she was here," Monica said. "Except we got a new mattress finally so company didn't break their backs. The lamp is different; I think the old one died. She used to sit at that desk and mark papers at night. I'd come in sometimes and we'd talk. She was like an older sister to me. Except we never fought."

"And she helped you with your homework," her mother said.

"She was a wonderful teacher. She had a gift for explaining things so they were clear. Everything she explained to me was easy to learn. I used to wish I could go to school in Studsburg."

We had informally sat down, mother and daughter on the bed, I on the desk chair. "Did she have visitors?" I asked.

They looked at each other. "Not that I recall," Mrs. Thurston said.

Monica shook her head in agreement.

"But she must have had friends."

"Well, I used to say that to her. I would say, 'Candy, a girl like you should go out with people your own age, even if it's only a movie on Saturday.' "

"But there was no one," I said.

"Well," the mother said. She looked at her daughter as though Monica were still too young to hear what was coming. "She fell in love, you know."

"She did?" Monica said.

Mrs. Thurston looked troubled. "He never came here for her. She would drive off and meet him somewhere."

"Did she confide in you?" I asked with hope.

"Only to say he was wonderful and special and older than she. And of course, I got the distinct impression that he wasn't available, if you know what I mean."

"She never said a word to me," said Monica, as though part of Candy's obligation under her lease had been to tell Monica all her secrets.

"Well, I wouldn't have expected it," her mother said. "It wasn't the kind of thing I would have wanted her to talk to you about. You were a child, and you had enough problems in your own life at that point that you didn't need any more."

I stood and took a last look around the room. As I started out, they followed me. The upstairs hall was covered in beige carpet, and there were family pictures on the walls. Monica had her own family now.

"Do you have any snapshots of Candy?" I asked as we went downstairs.

"I'll get the album," Mrs. Thurston said, and she went back up.

16

The pictures were old, but they were clear and sharp. They showed a girl with short, fluffy hair and a smile that could go a long way with interviewers. She always seemed to be moving. There was Candy, barefoot and in jeans, washing her car with young Monica, Candy getting out of the vintage Volkswagen, Candy jumping for a basketball, Candy and Mrs. Thurston carrying out food for a backyard picnic. There were also winter shots: Candy in a heavy coat and boots, shoveling the driveway, Candy and Monica making a snowman, Candy caught unawares reading a letter as she carried the mail to the house. Mrs. Thurston had not exaggerated Candy's helpfulness.

"She's awfully pretty," I said.

"And that was the least of it," Mrs. Thurston said. "It was that wonderful spirit she had."

"I want to be completely honest with you." I looked at both of them. "I've learned more from you than from anyone else I've talked to. I spoke to at least two men from Studsburg who knew Candy worked there that last year, and they said nothing about her, as though she didn't exist. I don't know why, and I think if I'm going to find out anything at all about who killed her, I need to know more."

"I'll tell you anything I can remember," Mrs. Thurston said. "But there isn't much more. I didn't know that much about her."

"Did she ever mention anything about her family? Her parents? Even her grandparents?" I still had the miraculous medal to explain, the initials A.M.

"Her mother had died, maybe a year or two before she came here, and she never ever talked about her father. I just assumed he'd died a long time before, maybe before she got to know him. She'd talk about high school sometimes, or maybe it was college, but if she mentioned any names, I forgot them a long time ago."

"Do you have any idea where she was going when she left Studsburg?"

Mrs. Thurston rested her chin on a hand as she tried to remember. "She did have a job, I'm sure of that. She started looking for one almost as soon as she got here."

"She went to Pennsylvania," Monica said. "I'm sure of it. She must have left us a forwarding address, Mom."

"Well, I just don't know. She said she'd get in touch when she was settled, and somehow I feel she fixed it up with the post office so I wouldn't have to do the forwarding."

And so letters with telltale return addresses wouldn't arrive at the house, I thought. "Did she leave at the end of the school year?"

"Around then, yes."

"And she took everything she had with her?"

"I guess so."

"Did she drive the old car?"

Mrs. Thurston looked uncertain. "I suppose she must have."

"She didn't, Mom. It broke down, don't you remember? Right at the end of the school year." Monica turned to me. "She'd only paid fifty dollars for it, and she got that back when she sold it."

"Who'd she sell it to?"

"A mechanic down at the garage. I remember going by and seeing those two windows in the back."

"So she took a bus or train wherever she was going when she left."

"She did, yes," Mrs. Thurston said. "I remember now. We drove her to the bus stop. Monica was with me. I had to fight back the tears."

"So you dropped her at a bus stop and never saw her again," I said. "Was that June or July, or isn't that a fair question after so many years?"

"It was after school let out. She had a chance for an apartment or a room somewhere, and she wanted to move in. I wish I could remember where. But that wasn't the last time we saw her. She came back for the Fourth of July."

"Tell me about it," I said.

"I remember!" Monica said excitedly. "She said she wanted to go to the big party at Studsburg. They were having fireworks that night."

Mrs. Thurston nodded her head. "That's right. She asked if she could stay just the one night, and I said sure, she could."

"Did she?" I asked, feeling a little breathless.

"Well, that's the whole thing. She came that afternoon, and I think I drove her over to Studsburg at some point, but she never came back."

"Did you look for her?" I asked.

"She told me . . . She said not to worry if she didn't get back before morning. I had the feeling she was going to see . . . you know . . . her friend for the last time, and maybe that's why she thought she'd be late. I was sure she'd be back, because she'd brought a little suitcase with her.''

"A duffel bag,'' Monica interrupted. "She had a little duffel with her when she came to the house.''

Her mother smiled. "So I was sure she'd be back, but when she didn't come the next day, I tried to call Studsburg, only all the phones were disconnected. Well, I left Monica by herself and I drove over there to see if I could find Candy.''

"Was anyone in town?''

"There were soldiers there, putting up one of those chain link fences. They certainly worked fast. I talked to a soldier, and he said everyone from town was gone. They'd been gone since noon. I should have called the police, shouldn't I?'' She looked pained, regretting a decision that would have made no difference anyway. Candy was probably dead and buried by the afternoon of the fifth.

"I understand your reluctance,'' I said.

"If she was with him . . . If he was looking after her . . .''

"I know.''

"It just seemed strange that she never came back for the duffel.''

"I bet we've still got it.'' Monica was on her feet. "Where would it be? The basement? The attic?''

I shared the excitement. She was jubilant, nearly jumping up and down.

"The attic,'' Monica said, running for the stairs. "I'm sure we'll find it.''

I followed them back up the stairs, nearly bursting with anticipation. In the center of the hall, Monica pulled a handle in the ceiling, and a flight of stairs floated down. We clambered up them as fast as we could.

The attic resembled my Aunt Meg's, a warehouse of unused and unusable objects, a collection of articles they couldn't bear to part with and probably never would, although they were no longer part of anyone's life.

"Those are my husband's golf clubs,'' Mrs. Thurston said,

"and the big umbrella I bought him for his last birthday. I couldn't ever bring myself to use it."

Monica was watching her mother with troubled eyes. I imagined her mother keeping all those feelings to herself, not wanting to upset a child any more than the death itself had upset her. Now, with the catalyst of Candy Phillips's mysterious departure, Mrs. Thurston had unlocked the inner door, dropped the guard of three decades, and let her feelings see the light of day—or at least the meager light of the attic. Maybe it was because I was there, a rational third person whose presence would keep a cap on their emotions.

"It would have kept you dry," the daughter said softly.

"I know. It was just a time when I would rather get wet."

We all stood there for a long moment, frozen in our places. Finally Mrs. Thurston picked up the huge black umbrella and handed it to her daughter. "Why don't you give it to Alan, dear? I'm sure he can use it."

Monica nodded and took the umbrella, tears in her eyes. She turned away and started looking for Candy Phillips's duffel bag. A moment later she said, "Here it is." Her voice was dispirited, as though her father's death had taken over her being. She lifted something off the floor, brushed it off, and handed it to me.

"Let's go downstairs," I said, and we all went down the floating ladder.

It was like opening a time capsule. The first thing I pulled out was a tube of Colgate toothpaste neatly turned up from the used bottom, the color flaking off the tube as I held it.

"When she didn't come back, I put all her things together," Mrs. Thurston said. "Her brush and comb and toothbrush and anything else I found up in her room. After I stopped worrying, I remember feeling angry, as though she'd betrayed our affection. I thought she must have run away with her boyfriend and forgotten all about us."

I reached back in and took out a bra, the elastic crumbling in my hand. It was a size 32B, and the label said Maidenform. The next thing out was her hairbrush. Just holding it gave me a chill. There were strands of ash blond hair in it, lighter than mine but not golden, Candy Phillips's own hair.

"That's just what her hair looked like," Monica said, her voice eerily low. "Everything about her was so natural. God, I can almost feel her in this room."

I could, too, as though in finding Candy's possessions, we had finally liberated her soul. There was a toothbrush in the bag, and a comb missing a couple of teeth. I found two pairs of underpants, one nylon and one cotton, both size five. The label on the nylon was gone, but the cotton ones were made by Lollipop. A cylindrical bottle of Ban deodorant with a little liquid still in the bottom was heavier than I expected. It turned out to be made of glass, not plastic. The contents of a small jar of colored cream was baked and cracked. The label said it was for facial eruptions. She had used about half of it before she closed it for the last time. If she owned any other makeup, it must have been in her handbag, which had not been buried with her, and I doubted anyone would ever find it.

There was a pair of short pajamas, one folded light blue T-shirt, and a pair of thick white socks with "Bonnie Doon" still faintly visible on the instep, but there were no stockings, no shoes, no dresses or skirts. She had worn a pair of jeans and had expected to wear them the day she left. Instead, she had died in them.

At the bottom of the bag there was an open box of ten regular Tampax. Perhaps she had carried a couple with her; perhaps she kept them in the duffel just in case, as I did. No one in the room said anything. If anything shows that you're young, female, and alive, it's a box of Tampax.

There was no jewelry of any kind in the duffel.

The last thing I pulled out was a copy of the *New Yorker* for the first week of July. It was opened to a short story Candy had never finished reading.

The contents of the bag lay in front of us on the coffee table. Monica picked up the brush and looked at it gravely.

"She'd be over fifty now, poor thing," Mrs. Thurston said. "Missed the best part of her life."

"Do either of you remember any jewelry she might have worn? Rings, bracelets, anything around her neck on a chain?"

"She had a watch," Mrs. Thurston said. "I don't remember what it looked like."

"No bracelets," Monica said. "I'm sure of that. I would have noticed."

I pulled my own chain out from inside my blouse. The miraculous medal I was given at birth was on it, along with my mother's and a cross I received as a child. Both women looked at it.

"She wasn't much for jewelry," Mrs. Thurston said. Which didn't rule out a chain that she might have worn, as I did, under her clothing.

"She had a string of some kind of beads," Monica said. "She used to wear them sometimes when she taught." She shrugged. "That's all I remember."

I started to put the things back in the bag when I felt something along the bottom. It was a small key chain made of little metal balls with a fastener connecting the two ends, the kind you can pick up in a dime store. Dangling from it was a miniature New York State license plate in black and orange. I held it up.

Monica nearly exploded. "It's Candy's license plate! Look, Mom, it's the little license plate I always loved." I gave it to her, and she started to cry as she looked at it. "It came in the mail," she said, "from one of those organizations that asks for money. She sent them a dollar for it. I remember, I remember. Oh, how could anyone have killed her?"

When she gave the key chain back, I repacked the duffel bag. "I'm not sure what to do with this. It's evidence in a homicide, and I suppose it ought to be turned over to the sheriff's office."

"He's such a bag of wind," Monica said. "Did you see him on TV trying to outplay the coroner?"

I said I had.

"You don't want him to have it, do you?" her mother said.

"I'd rather wait. I'd hate to see Candy's death become a political circus."

"Well, why don't you leave that bag right here then? I'll put it back in the attic and we'll all forget about it. When you're ready, we can just find it again."

I thanked her, and she gave me a hug. I left my phone numbers with her and promised she'd hear from me. As we all walked out to my car, I said, "Did you ever know a woman named Beadles who had a daughter named Joanne?"

Mrs. Thurston recognized the name first. "There was a Ginny Beadles who worked in the coffee shop, but that was a long time ago. Didn't she marry the owner, Monica?"

"She could've. But it's changed hands a lot. You think she married Pop?"

"No, the one before him. It was Mike and Millie's Place, and Mike and Millie split up." She laughed. "We're just full of scandals around here."

"I don't suppose you remember Mike's last name."

"No. Don't think I ever knew it. But I knew Ginny Beadles because she worked for a time in the bank, and there was a little sign at her window with her name on it."

"She left the bank for a waitressing job?"

"I think she had her eye on Mike." Mrs. Thurston laughed again.

"Did you know her daughter?"

"I don't think I even knew she had one."

"Thank you both," I said. As I drove away I felt it had been more exhausting for them than for me.

17

It was late enough in the afternoon that I could call Mrs. Mulholland's daughter, Amy Broderick. I found a pay phone at the gas station in the center of town and called her number. She had spoken to her mother and knew who I was.

"Are you down in Studsburg now?" she asked.

"Not too far away. I've been talking to people in the area today, and I have some questions about your last teacher there."

"Miss Phillips?"

"That's the one."

"Can you tell me why?"

"She's been missing for a long time, and I'm trying to find out what happened to her."

"I don't know anything that happened after we left Studsburg."

"It's the year in Studsburg I'm interested in."

"Will you still be around tomorrow?"

"Yes, I will."

"My husband and I have been meaning to drive down and see the town. He's never been there. Could I meet you at the church tomorrow morning, say eleven?"

"That would be great."

"I'll have a surprise for you," she said. "Look for us about eleven. We'll be two excited adults and two reluctant kids—if I can get my sixteen-year-old to come along."

I promised I'd be there.

* * *

The nuns at Sacred Heart couldn't quite believe it. Last night I hadn't had the faintest idea whose body had been buried in the church, and this evening I knew with absolute certainty. It had been largely luck, I assured them, a chance call to a woman who had lived there.

"More than chance," Sister Concepta said. "Someone lied to you, and you were following up on that lie. Now all you have to do is find the killer."

I couldn't help laughing. "All I have to do," I echoed.

"It shouldn't be too hard. It's one of those people who lied. And you're welcome here till you find out which one."

For that, I assured her, I was very grateful.

I left after breakfast Saturday morning, taking my suitcase with me. I would return Sunday evening after Jack went back to New York, but in the meantime there were several things I wanted to do; more, in fact, than I had time for. My first destination was the post office in the Thurstons' town. I couldn't think of any other way of finding out where Candy Phillips had gone to when she left at the end of the school year, and I wanted to know why no one had been concerned when she failed to arrive. I didn't really have much hope that the post office would keep a forwarding address for thirty years, but I had to start somewhere.

Raised eyebrows and a look more suspicious than quizzical greeted my questions. "Thirty years? We only forward mail a year."

"I know that, but maybe you have a record somewhere."

"Miss, this building wasn't here thirty years ago. And if you want to know the truth, neither was I."

"Could you point me to an old-timer?"

He stared at me a few seconds before moving away. Then I heard him call, "Anyone know where Tom is?"

Tom materialized eventually, a man probably nearing retirement. I hoped he'd made a career of the post office.

"Tell me what you're looking for," he said, "and I'll see what I can do."

I told him. He listened. At one point he said, "Thurston, yeah. I know the name. But I don't remember anything about a forwarding address."

"Maybe the forwarding card is filed away somewhere. I wouldn't mind looking through them myself. And I know the month and year."

"Lotta old stuff got thrown out when we moved into the new building."

"Is there someplace we could look? Just on the chance that it's there?"

"Could you tell me why it's so all-fired important?"

I really couldn't take him into my confidence, and I have a tough time lying, which has made me rather inventive with the truth. "She's a very important person to me, and she's been missing for thirty years. I've traced her this far, and right here I've reached a dead end. I don't know where to go from here." I hoped, if he had any imagination at all, that he would assume I was an illegitimate child trying to trace her mother. Certainly the years were right. I met his eyes.

"Come with me." He said it abruptly as though he were irritated or, possibly, moved.

We went downstairs to a basement filled with file boxes and cartons.

"I don't even know where to start," Tom said.

I wasn't going to let him get away with that. Taking the initiative, I walked over to the nearest carton and looked at the year scrawled on the top. Under it was a carton a couple of years older. I looked at one in a nearby stack. Older still. "Toward that wall," I said, pointing.

He got into the act, and I helped him jockey the cartons around.

Finally he said, "You sure of the date?"

"Positive."

"Look in this one."

The rubber bands that had held the old cards together had long since disintegrated, and everything in the carton was a mess. There was no chronological order or any other order that I could figure out. So I just took it piece by piece, item by item, until I found it.

"It's here," I said jubilantly.

"You really got it?"

"I really do."

The old address was c/o Thurston at their home. The new address was a town in Pennsylvania that I had never heard of. And printed along the bottom of the slip was the message: PLEASE DO NOT DELIVER MAIL TO THE THURSTON ADDRESS. That, I decided, was to prevent the Thurstons from seeing who her mail came from. Her lover must have had a highly recognizable name—or address.

Tom took the card from me and scratched his head. "It's coming back," he said. "It was a long time ago. We called her the musical-chairs girl. You know how to play musical chairs?"

"Sort of."

"The mail came here, we forwarded it; coupla weeks later, it's back, readdressed by the addressee."

"You mean when they got it, they sent it back here?"

"That's what they did. But we had no place to send it here, so we sent it back there again. Musical chairs."

Tom seemed pretty pleased with himself, and suddenly reluctant to go upstairs and resume work. But I had no more time for chitchat. I was meeting Amy Broderick at St. Mary Immaculate in half an hour.

The sixteen-year-old had not been persuaded to come. The Brodericks were a good-looking couple with a twelve-year-old son playing with a hand-held game. Amy Broderick waved husband and son away when she identified me, and we walked into the church together. She was a small woman wearing pants and boots and carrying a handsome bag over her shoulder. She opened it as soon as we were inside.

"I went over to my mother's last night for this. My mother is one of those superorganized women who can put her hand on anything in two seconds flat. Look."

It was a folder with a class picture. Standing in the center of the back row was Candy Phillips. A hand-lettered sign held by the two children in the middle of the front row gave the year and class. There were only two rows, eight smiling, well-scrubbed children about to enter their teens and the legendary decade of the sixties.

"You haven't changed," I said.

"Well, I don't weigh eighty pounds anymore."

But pretty close, I estimated. "This is really great," I said.

"If you promise I'll get it back, I'll let you have it."

"You'll get it back."

"What do you want to know about Miss Phillips?"

"Anything you remember."

"I adored her." She laughed. "That's the whole story. If anyone was responsible for my wanting to be a teacher, it was Miss Phillips. It wasn't an easy job. She had three classes and she was replacing someone who'd been there for years, but she eased into it as though she'd been made for us. She was probably the first young teacher Studsburg had had in twenty years. And she was wonderful."

"Did you ever see her outside of school?"

"Oh, sure. She'd go to the coffee shop in the afternoon sometimes until it closed down or do some shopping at the store. We were kind of giggly at that age, but she was always so nice to us. You'd see her little car parked here and there. If it was on Main Street, you knew she was in one of the shops there."

"The newspaper had an office on Main Street, too, didn't it?"

"Everything was on Main Street."

"I know you were young, but children often notice things, even things they aren't expected to see. Did you ever see her with a man?"

"You mean like a boyfriend?"

"Maybe."

"Not that I can remember. But I was only eleven. I wasn't

out much at night, except to go to baseball games. She went
to those, too. You'd see her car in the lot near the field. You
couldn't miss it. It was an old Volkswagen with two little
windows in the back. I bet it's in a museum now.''

Her husband and son waved as they passed. They had been
downstairs, probably to see where the body was found. It
struck me that if you drove a distinctive car in a very small
town, you couldn't very well park in front of your lover's
house or everyone would know about it in ten minutes. But
if you parked in front of the grocery store and walked down
the block to where the newspaper was published, people
would assume you were in the grocery store. And if you
parked near the baseball field, you could easily slip away to
the wooded area that was nearby. I remembered the aerial
photograph of the town that Fred Larkin had showed me. He
had pointed out the playing field and then moved the pointer
just a bit to show me the woods where he had proposed to
his wife. It wasn't a big town, and you could probably walk
from one end to the other in less than twenty minutes.

''Do you remember where that baseball field was?'' I
asked.

''Sure.'' I followed as she walked away from the downtown area. ''You can't see anything now that would give you
a clue, but it was over that way where it's pretty flat. We had
bleachers and everything. My brother used to play ball
there.''

''And wasn't there a wooded section somewhere near it?''

''That was off to the right. Let's see. Look at that. I think
they've left all the tree stumps there.'' She pointed, and I
saw them for the first time, like a field of piles. ''It was very
beautiful in the summer, very lush.''

''You said your brother played ball. Is he older than you?''

''Two years. He was in the eighth grade that year. He was
the last class to graduate from Studsburg.''

''Do you think he'd talk to me.''

''Jerry? Sure. Why wouldn't he? He was a terror, my

brother. But he doesn't live upstate anymore. He lives near New York."

"So do I," I said.

She took a small notebook out of her bag, flipped it open, and wrote on it. "You know, when I went over to pick up the class picture last night, my mother said something very odd. She said she wished she hadn't mentioned that school-teacher to you—she'd forgotten Miss Phillips's name—that it could only stir up trouble. Do you have any idea what she was talking about?"

"Not yet, but I hope I will pretty soon."

"That was a funny year as I remember it," Amy said as she handed me the slip of paper with her brother's name and phone numbers. "My father was already working in Roch-ester, which was a terrible commute, but they stayed in Studsburg till the end. They had put the house up for sale for a while when my father started commuting, but they didn't sell it. I guess they stayed because they wanted Jerry to grad-uate." She laughed. "Maybe they were afraid no other school would have him."

"I'd appreciate your doing me a small favor," I said. "Please don't tell your mother I intend to talk to your brother about Miss Phillips."

"There is something funny going on, isn't there?"

"All I know is, I haven't been able to find an adult to talk about her, even people who were responsible for her coming to Studsburg."

"I wonder why."

Her husband and son turned the corner of the back of the church and waved. As they got close, the boy said, "You should go down there, Mom. What a weird place that is where they found the body."

"I'll be right with you," Amy said. She turned to me to shake hands and stopped, her hand raised. "You think that body in the church was Miss Phillips, don't you?"

"I'm sure of it."

"My God. And you think my parents know something about it?"

"They know something; I don't know what. It's something that seems to everyone's benefit to keep secret. If I can find out why, maybe I'll find out who killed her."

She shook hands with me at last, and I took it to mean that she would not alert her parents.

"Will you let me know?" she said.

"I promise."

18

I had sat in my spare, quiet room at the convent last night trying to figure out how to find Virginia Beadles. *If* she had married in the area, I might be able to locate her marriage license. But to do so, I might have to go through fifteen or twenty years of licenses. Since the ownership of the coffee shop had changed more than once since her marriage, I decided that was likely to be a dead end. Instead, I made it to the one bank in town minutes before they closed at noon.

I was getting pretty skilled at locating the oldest person present, and I made for a gray head at a desk. He turned out to be the manager, but he had no idea who Virginia Beadles was.

"When did you say she worked here?"

"I'm not sure, but it could have been as much as thirty years ago."

"Well, I've been here for eight, and as I look around, I don't see anyone who has that kind of longevity."

"Maybe one of the tellers would remember someone who retired and still lives in the area," I suggested.

"Good idea."

I waited while he asked an older woman who was putting things in order. Even at a distance I could see her smile. He came back to his desk with something written on a scrap of paper.

"I hope you're not a bill collector," he said.

"I'm just trying to find Ginny Beadles. We have a connection from a long time ago."

He dialed, and I listened to him make easy conversation with a stranger, something I have never learned to do. Finally he told her he had a "a lady here who's trying to find Virginia Beadles, but she doesn't know her new last name." He listened, and I could hear the voice in his earpiece. He wrote something, said a few more comfortable phrases, and hung up.

"There you go." He pushed the paper toward me. "I'd guess she lives about twenty minutes from here."

I almost said, "Thanks a bunch," but I couldn't quite form the words.

Virginia Beadles had become Mrs. Mike Carpenter. I took a chance and drove there.

There are places in this country where you don't have to be rich to own a house. Where land is plentiful, it is often cheap, and old houses they call a "fixer-upper" or a "handyman's special" go for a song. The house the Carpenters lived in needed a carpenter without the capital. It needed a couple of coats of paint and probably some structural work. The front porch sagged, and you would have had a hard time finding a line that was perpendicular to the ground. Still, it had two stories, and I guessed it was more comfortable to live in than an apartment. A thin woman with very blond hair was picking up in the front yard when I parked at the edge of the road. She was wearing gray pants and old sneakers with a black jacket zipped up to the neck. She looked up and watched me approach.

"You lost?" she said.

"I hope not. I'm looking for Virginia Carpenter."

"That's me. I win the lottery or something?"

"Not that I know of. My name is Chris Bennett. I'm really looking for your daughter, Joanne."

Her face sobered. "I don't know what you mean. I don't have a daughter."

"Joanne Beadles," I said.

"What's your business here?"

"Mrs. Carpenter, a body was found a couple of weeks ago in the church in Studsburg."

"That's not my daughter," she said quickly.

"How do you know?"

"What makes you think it's Joanne?"

"It isn't Joanne," I said. "I know that."

"Who the hell are you?"

"I'm a friend of some people who lived in Studsburg. I'm trying to find out who the woman was who was buried in the church. The sheriff isn't trying very hard."

"The sheriff never tries very hard except when he's up for election."

"Could we talk about Joanne?"

She looked at her left wrist, which was empty. "You got the time? My watch is broke."

"It's one."

"He'll be back soon. I can't talk when he's here."

"If he comes, I'll say I saw your milk can out front and I wondered if it was for sale."

"It ain't."

We went inside. Before she sat down, she added wood to an iron stove in the corner of the living room. As I watched, the flames became visible through a small glass window in the front of the stove. She did something and a fan went on, carrying the warmth to the sofa where I was sitting.

"Is your daughter alive, Mrs. Carpenter?" I asked when she had sat down.

"Of course she's alive. Why wouldn't she be?"

"Can you tell me where she is?"

She looked down at the floor. The roots of her short blond hair were completely gray and her face was lined, although I didn't think she was even seventy. "No, I can't tell you. And I don't want to talk about it."

"I want to know about J.J. Eberling."

"I don't know about him. She worked for his wife."

"Do you remember for how long?"

"A few months. Maybe more."

"Did she talk to you about it?"

"She didn't talk to me about anything."

"But she was living at home at that time, wasn't she?"

She didn't answer. She reached for a pack of cigarettes and lit one, blowing smoke away from me, but the current of hot air from the wood stove brought it gently back. "She lived with me. For a while."

"And then?"

"He got her a place to live."

"Mr. Eberling?"

"Who else? We didn't know the kind of people who could pay for extra apartments."

"Why do you think he did that, Mrs. Carpenter?"

"Why do you think? Do I have to draw you a picture? She was his—" She broke off and inhaled sharply. It was almost a sob. She drew on the cigarette and turned to me, smoke issuing from her mouth. "Did you ever lose a child, Miss Bennett?"

"I lost a mother. When I was about your daughter's age."

"That can be rough," she said. "I know. Joanne didn't lose me. It was the other way around."

"You think she was his girlfriend."

"It doesn't make it any nicer to put it that way. He was keeping her. A man thirty years older than her."

"Did you ever ask her about it?"

"Sure I asked her. She was my daughter. She said she knew how to push him around and she told him she wanted to have her own place to live and he gave it to her."

"Maybe it was true," I said.

She smiled bitterly. "Sure. A nineteen-year-old kid knows how to push around a rich man and make him spend money on her. Only one way I know to do that."

"You think she was pregnant?"

"I don't know what I think."

"Where is she, Mrs. Carpenter?"

"I don't know."

"But you're sure she's alive."

"I'm not sure of anything anymore. I just know she was alive the last time I saw her."

"When was that?"

She puffed on the cigarette. "She came back to me one day. Looked nice, had a nice outfit on. She was a nice-lookin' kid, my Joanne. She said she was goin' away. Wouldn't say where, just she was goin' away. She asked if I wanted to come with her."

"She invited you to come along?"

"You could call it inviting me, yeah. She said the Eberlings were movin' out of town—they were gonna flood it, everybody knew that—and she couldn't work for them anymore. So she was leavin'. I said, 'Tell me what's goin' on, Joanne. What's goin' on with you and that man? I won't get mad at you, just tell me.' She said it was nothing."

"And that was it? She just left?"

"She gave me something." She tamped out the cigarette in the ashtray next to her.

I waited for her to go on, but she didn't. "What did she give you?" I said finally.

"Money."

"I see."

"A lotta money. She pulled it out of her purse like she had it ready in case I said I wouldn't go with her. It was ten hundreds. A thousand bucks."

"That was a great deal of money."

"You know how long I had to work to make a thousand bucks?"

"A long time." If Studsburg was paying a teacher four thousand, it was a cinch the bank was paying a lot less than that for tellers.

"Anyway, that was it. She said good-bye, no kiss, no nothin'. Just good-bye. I never saw her again."

"Did you report her missing?" I asked. I already knew she hadn't. Deputy Drago had checked that.

"I called the police without giving my name. I asked how you report a missing person. The cop said you had to wait a coupla days because most people show up. Then he asked how old the person was, and when I said nineteen, he said you know adults can go where they please. I got the feeling he wasn't too anxious to look for anyone if he could get out of it."

"So that was it."

"No, that wasn't it," she said irritably. "That was my kid, my only child, and I loved her, believe it or not. I said some things to her that last time I shouldn'ta said and I was sorry for it, but it was too late to take it back. I wanted to find her. So I went to the Eberlings—I found their new house, I don't remember how—and I said I was Joanne's mother and I wanted to know where she was. The woman was there and she said Joanne had quit a couple of weeks ago and they hadn't seen her since. So I came back at night when I figured he'd be there and I said I knew about the apartment and I knew about what was going on and I wanted to know where my daughter was."

I felt a surge of admiration for this woman who had obviously been alone in the world, obviously cared for her daughter, and had fought off her intimidations to confront a local god. "What did he say?" I asked.

"He said if I pursued this nonsense—that's just how he put it—if I pursued this, he would get his lawyers after me, he would sue me for everything I had, and he would see to it that I never worked in this area again. He was a big guy— at least he looked pretty big to me, standing there in front of this house of theirs—and I'll tell you, he scared the shit outa me. I couldn't afford a lawyer, I couldn't prove anything. All I knew was my daughter was gone and I had a thousand dollars in cash she'd given me. That was it. And the cops weren't too anxious to help. What would you have done?''

''I don't know.''

''I kept the money for a long time. I figured she'd be back when she needed it. But she never did come back. So when Mike and me bought this house, I put it into the down payment.'' She waved her hand toward the wall. ''So that's it. You're lookin' at it.''

''And you never heard from her again?''

''Not a phone call. Not a Christmas card. It's true, she didn't know I got married, so if she looked me up, I'm not in the book anymore, and they don't forward letters forever.''

That was something I knew myself. ''Did you know the apartment where she was living?''

Ginny Carpenter nodded without looking at me. ''I followed her. She didn't have a car, so I figured it couldn't be too far. There were some old garden apartments in town. She had a place there.''

She described where they were, and I wrote it down. I didn't think I could get much more information from her, and I had my own life to think about this afternoon, so I thanked her and put my coat on. The room had become wonderfully warm, the heat from the stove permeating the space.

At the door she put her hand on the knob but didn't open it. ''If you find her, will you let me know?''

''Of course.''

''I don't know if she wants to see me—''

''I'll tell you whatever I find out.''

''Thanks,'' she said.

A Bronco was just pulling into the gravel drive as I got to my car.

The route to the motel where I was meeting Jack took me right back through the town where the garden apartments were. I stopped and found the manager's office. The woman who came to the door was too young to have known Joanne Beadles, but I tried anyway. As it turned out, she was the daughter of the former owners, and most of the tenants had lived there so long that the turnover was very light.

"She was the youngest girl that ever lived here," she said. "Most of our people are older and stay forever. She didn't stay long."

"Did she have company?"

"Honey, I can't tell you who had company last night. You really think I can remember that far back? We don't pry as long as people are quiet."

"I assume she paid her bills," I said, trying another tack.

"She must have or my mother wouldn't have kept her."

"What I'd like to know most of all is where she went when she left."

"I don't know how I could find that out. We don't forward mail or anything like that."

"Do you think your mother might remember?" I'd come further than I expected, and I just couldn't accept failure when I sensed I was close to success.

"I suppose I could . . ." She stopped, something occurring to her. "You know what? We probably sent her a check for her security after she moved. My mother never handed out a check right away, because you could find they did damage that you didn't see at first, like scratching the floor or making holes in the walls. Let me check the book for you."

She had been right about the small turnover, because the book she opened was marked "1957–" and no concluding date. She turned pages near the beginning.

"Here she is, Joanne Beadles. She was paying seventy dollars a month, and my mother sent her a check for sixty-five. She wrecked the paint with masking tape in a couple of places, and we had to touch it up. She moved to New York. Want the address?"

"You bet," I said. I had my notebook open and wrote it

down. Joanne had moved into an apartment in midtown Manhattan on the west side, a neighborhood that has undergone some upheavals since the sixties, not all of them for the better.

"I couldn't tell you if she cashed the check, but that's where we sent it. It's kind of a long time, isn't it?"

"It's a start," I said, and went to meet Jack.

19

"That was worth the trip." Jack had his arms around me, and everything, from the way I felt, to the closeness of his body, to the comfort of the hotel bed compared to the narrow, thin mattress at the convent, felt good.

"I'm glad you got here early," I said.

"Could I talk you into a drink in the bar downstairs?"

"You could talk me into anything right now."

"Lemme get my list."

I laughed. It was good to talk to someone close to me, someone I didn't have to explain my motives to. After spending days listening for hidden secrets and unintended disclosures, after taking notes so I could reconstruct conversations that might offer something new on a second or third mental hearing, it was a pleasure to engage in banter after the kind of sex that occurs when you think you can't wait for it a minute longer. It had been that kind, and my spirits were high.

The bar was almost empty. I haven't been to many bars in my life, although I'm not a stranger to alcohol, but from my handful of recent experiences, I've decided I like them better empty and quiet than full and noisy. The TV set in this one had the sound turned off, and anyway we sat at a table where we couldn't see it. Jack ordered vodka, Stoly on the rocks, and I got a whiskey sour, which would hold me for a long time. Then we talked a little, touched hands, kissed a couple of times.

"I got a B," he said finally.

"In the test? That's good. That's wonderful. You worry too much."

"If I don't worry, I don't work hard. You want me to ask how it's going?"

"Ask away."

"Solve the homicide yet?"

"I'm not even sure how many homicides there were. But I know whose body I found in the church. I haven't told the sheriff yet."

"Probably won't make much difference unless he's up for election. You pin it on anyone?"

"I've got two, maybe three suspects, but nothing holds together. There's no obvious motive. Her name was Candida Phillips and she was a schoolteacher, just hired for the last year of the town's existence. Her landlady told me Candy fell in love with someone that year, an older man who was probably married. Two older married men who had interviewed her for the job 'forgot' she worked in town that year, and one of them warned the other one I was on my way to his house. The second one, the former mayor, lied about who was teaching that year."

"So they know something. Could one of them have done it?"

"Either one of them could have. They were both at the Fourth of July town picnic, and they were probably at the fireworks that night. It wouldn't have been too hard to slip away, meet her downstairs in the church, and shoot her during the fireworks. I think that's how it happened, a shot during the fireworks."

"And then what?"

"And then he stuffed her body in the opening, sealed it up, and came back outside."

"When did he open up the place where he was going to bury her? That had to take time. You don't do that in ten minutes flat."

"I don't know. Maybe during the afternoon after Maddie's baptism."

He looked at his watch. "Drink up. Let's run over there while it's light."

"I got you interested," I said.

"I was interested from the start. I just didn't have the time to think about it."

There were still some people milling around the town, especially around St. Mary Immaculate. On the short drive over I had told Jack about J.J. Eberling, who had to fit into this somehow, although the strongest connection I could find was the missing last issue of the *Studsburg Herald*. Whether Joanne Beadles figured into anything connected with Candy Phillips's murder, I just couldn't say.

We went down the stairs on the left-hand side of the church as I had two weeks earlier at almost the same time of day.

"See how the back of the church is curved? That's why I couldn't see whoever it was who was at the opening."

"But you could hear him."

I thought about it. "I didn't really hear him moving the rock or scraping around. He must have done that earlier. What I heard was a ping, something metallic falling. I haven't told you about that." I took it out of my change purse and handed it to him. "It's a miraculous medal. Look at the date."

He whistled. "More'n ninety years old."

"It doesn't fit anyone who lived in Studsburg. There was only one person with the initials A.M., Amy Mulholland, and she was eleven years old at the time. She's Amy Broderick now, and I met her this morning."

"You really have been busy."

We walked along the hall till we came to the opening. A few people stood in front of it, making comments on the murder. We waited till they went up the stairs and then moved closer.

"It looked to me as though her hand was pointing out," I said. "Maybe she was clutching the medal. I think it may be what he came back for."

"Hard to believe she could have hung on to it for thirty years, Chris. There couldn't've been any flesh left."

"Then he could've found it on the floor, picked it up, and dropped it when I called."

"You called?"

I thought about it to get the chronology right. "No, I heard the ping first. Then I called, just to let whoever it was know that someone was there. That's when he took off up those steps." I indicated the ones just beside us.

"So he knows you were there and he knows the sheriff doesn't have the medal or he would have said something about it."

"You're telling me he knows I have it."

"Seems kind of obvious."

"But he doesn't know who I am, Jack."

"He could have gotten your plate number."

"It's possible," I said. "My impression was, he just got away as fast as he could."

"I worry about you, Chris."

That gave me a nice chill. I got down on my haunches beside him. The police had cleaned the opening out, scraping all the gook off the floor. Jack tried to move the stone. I could see it wasn't easy.

"He had to have tools to open this up," he said.

"He took them with him. I heard a metallic clatter before he ran, and there wasn't anything here when I got here."

"And he knew exactly what he was looking for."

I looked at the miraculous medal. "Which means it identifies him. If I could only figure out how."

We went up the stairs and outside. I showed Jack where

the athletic field had been, where the woods were where Fred Larkin had proposed to his wife, where Main Street was. We walked over and looked at the bridge.

"Somewhere around there, J.J. Eberling was handing out the *Studsburg Herald* that last day until he changed his mind."

"Something made him change it."

We left the Main Street bridge and walked back toward the church.

"Something was going on in that town, Jack," I said. "When I met Amy this morning, she said her mother said she was sorry she'd ever mentioned that teacher. Somehow Candy Phillips was involved with someone in Studsburg, like the mayor or J.J. Eberling, and there's a wall of silence around them. The only way I can think to break through are with people who didn't live in town or with the children."

"Who are now adults."

"But they haven't been warned to keep quiet. I've got Amy's brother's phone number. He lives near New York and he was in Candy's eighth grade."

"Maybe that's the way to go." He gave me his hand as we mounted the slope.

In the car I took out the sixth grade class picture that Amy had given me that morning and showed it to him in the glow of the dome light.

He held it for a long time, looking at Candy's smiling face. "That's when it breaks your heart," he said.

Maybe that's why I loved him.

We found a nice restaurant for dinner, and I told him the rest of what I knew. He took down Joanne Beadles's name and thirty-year-old address and said he'd do what he could to locate her. Then I gave him the names and Studsburg addresses of the two men who seemed to be hiding something from me, Larkin and Degenkamp, and for good measure, J.J. Eberling's as well. I wanted to know if any of them had owned a .38-caliber handgun on the Fourth of July thirty years ago. While he was writing everything down, he said he'd also check Candy's pension with Albany.

Although I spent a lot of time telling him what I knew, I listened very carefully to his questions. Jack is always concerned with the kind of details I tend to push away because I can't explain them, hoping they'll just drop into place by themselves. The opening in the wall was a big problem for him. The stone was heavy, and although it could be moved by one person—he had done it himself as I watched—there was obvious preparation involved in using that opening as a grave. At the very least, the stone had to have been loosened before the homicide, and tools had to be used to accomplish it. Otherwise, the killer would have been gone from the picnic or fireworks for a very long time.

"Maybe he was," I said. "Maybe they're all covering for him."

"But why?"

"Maybe they liked him. Maybe they hated Candy for some reason."

"Maybe she found out something she wasn't supposed to know."

"Something you could kill for?"

"Chris, somebody put a bullet in her. Find out why and you'll probably find out who. You said she may have had a married lover. Maybe she was pregnant."

"She wasn't."

He looked at me without asking.

"The coroner thought she wasn't, but I found something that really convinced me. She had an open box of Tampax in the duffelbag she carried. If you go away for a day or two and just pack underwear and socks, you don't bother putting in your Tampax if you're pregnant."

"Agreed. So he wanted to break it off, and she was threatening to tell his wife."

Mayor Larkin? Henry Degenkamp? But Ellie Degenkamp was in on the secret, whatever it was. And if it had been her husband, she wouldn't have had to prompt him not to talk about it. He would have known that himself. J.J. Eberling? Certainly something had happened between him and Joanne Beadles. Had it happened with Candy, too, only she couldn't be bought off?

"I feel like I know so much and there are still so many questions," I said.

"You do know a lot. You're probably miles ahead of the sheriff."

"The sheriff and I care about different things."

He put his hand over mine. "What do you care about?"

"I'm so glad you came upstate today," I said.

We got back to the hotel in that sweet, lazy haze that a good meal and some wine seem to conjure up. Everything I had imagined about hotel rooms turned out to be true. Somehow when you close the door and there's nothing except that big bed and the guy you're crazy about, the soporific effect of the wine easily transforms into a need, a slow burn, an ache to couple, even if it's what you did this afternoon.

Jack is the first man in my life, the only one. I don't know how it would be with anyone else, and when I'm with him, I don't care. Even when I'm not with him, I don't care. What we do together is very right and very special.

20

The motel had a good Sunday brunch starting at eleven. Jack and I are both early risers, and we decided to spend a couple of hours using our muscles. We drove to the river near Studsburg, parked, and started walking upstream, away from the dam that had been built to flood the town.

Most of the land was farmland with very few buildings, just an occasional farmhouse and barn. Next to almost every house was a huge dish to aid television reception. The river that in normal times supplied the water that created the lake that had been Studsburg was well down from its banks. The drought had been going on for two years, and I wondered how the farmers were faring. We stopped walking finally as the land began to slope downward, neither of us wanting to climb back up once we got to the bottom. Instead, we turned around and went back to where we'd parked. From there, Jack drove in the other direction, to the dam that had been built thirty years earlier. Today there was barely a trickle coming through.

"They built it for flood control," I said. "Instead of indiscriminate flooding, they directed the water into the Studsburg basin. Look at it now."

"You can deal with a problem, but you can't forecast it. It'll rain again; you can be sure of that."

Almost as sure as that the sun would set this day, that we would kiss and say good-bye, that we would hunger for each other. We got back to the motel with just enough time to change for brunch.

I decided to use the phone in the room before we checked out rather than add to my growing debt at the convent. I took my list out and found Father Hartman's number. He was in the rectory and came to the phone.

"I have something to tell you in confidence," I said.

"Is it about the body in the church?"

"I think I know who it was. The town hired a teacher for the top three grades for that last year."

"That's right. Mr. Dietrich left for another job. She was new at teaching, but she did very well. Phillips," he said.

"Then you knew her."

"I knew her, I knew Mrs. McCormick, I knew them all. Are you telling me someone murdered her?"

"I think so. Father, I heard that J.J. Eberling used the rectory after his Main Street office was closed down."

"That's true, but we rarely saw each other. I gave him a room on the ground floor that I never used, and usually I wasn't aware of whether he was in it or not. Sometimes I'd hear his typewriter clacking—he wrote a column, you know, besides editing the paper.''

"I heard.''

"But if it was quiet, I had no way of knowing if he was there. People would drop by to leave their stories, but it was like a separate little business. We didn't interfere with each other.''

"Father, I know about Darlene Jackson and Joanne Beadles.''

He was quiet. Then he said, "I knew you would hear. As far as I'm concerned, it was all rumor. No one ever talked to me about it. No one ever brought charges.''

"Do you think J.J. could have killed Candy Phillips?''

"You're asking for my opinion. I don't think he did. And beyond that, I never heard a whisper connecting him to her.''

"Just one more thing," I said. "Do you have any recollection of a Studsburger with the initials A.M. who was born in 1898?''

"In 1898," he repeated. "Someone in his sixties when the town ended. Offhand, I can't think of anyone.''

"Could it have been someone who left town a couple of years earlier?''

"Tell you what. I carried all the church records to the chancery when I left Studsburg. I'll take a run up there and go through the baptismal records.''

"I'd really appreciate that." I had assumed they were put away safely somewhere. Records of baptisms and marriages are often used to establish facts that may not be recorded by government agencies or have been lost. People really rely on church records.

We had to check out soon, and I wanted to spend some time with Jack before he left. As I picked up my address list to put it in my bag, something just below "Hartman" caught my eye. Mayor Fred Larkin, wife Gwen. I stared at the name.

"Her name isn't Gwen," I said aloud.

"Whose?"

"The mayor's wife. He called her Evvie. He said Evvie didn't like his smoking. She's Gwen on the list."

"So he changed wives. Lots of guy do it."

"Jack, Carol Stifler keeps this list updated. She wouldn't forget to change the name of the mayor's wife. And that's not all." I was feeling excited. When you discover someone's been lying to you, it gets the juices going. "He talks as though there's only been one wife. He told me he'd met her in the eighth grade. He didn't say 'my first wife,' he said 'my wife.' That isn't something I could have gotten wrong. He's keeping it secret that he's not married to Gwen anymore."

"OK, so he got divorced, and in his generation, you don't do that kind of thing. Is he Catholic?"

"Yes. He was married in St. Mary Immaculate."

"So that's it. He did something the church says he shouldn't have, and he's ashamed. He doesn't want all his old friends to know about it."

I ran it through my mind. Sometimes people are called by one name early in their lives and by another later because the first name goes out of fashion. But as I conjured up the image of Evvie Larkin, I could now see what hadn't really made an impression on me when I met her, that she was younger than her husband, substantially younger. He could never have met Evvie in eighth grade, because she would have been in kindergarten, and eighth graders don't hold hands with little kids. "He's hiding something," I said aloud. "It's what one of the nuns said. There are three liars. One of them is a killer, or protecting a killer."

Jack looked suddenly very sober. "When you get that look, I get the feeling you're on to something."

"Something's wrong there, Jack. Maybe this is the break I've been waiting for."

"Can I escort you back to the convent before I leave? To make sure you get there in one piece?"

I couldn't help laughing. "No, you can't. And don't make me promise to keep out of trouble."

"I'm calling you there tonight."

"OK."

"And you're calling me tomorrow when you get home."

"I will."

"And if I don't hear from you, I'll have the state police out looking for you. I'm not kidding, Chris."

"You'll hear from me."

After Jack left, I drove back to the convent. Several of the nuns had visitors, and a number of people were crowding into the shop. I went to the kitchen to offer my help, but it was too late to scrape vegetables for dinner, and all the breakfast dishes had been washed and put away hours ago. I didn't feel much like sitting in my small room, so I walked over to the chapel and sat in a pew. A family was walking through, looking at the windows and the altar. The wife was carrying a bag with the name of the convent on it, so I knew they had bought some preserves. They talked in the low tones people often reserve for churches and they smiled at me as they passed, feeling the friendship of strangers visiting the same place.

When they left, I lighted my three candles and went back to the pew. Alone, I planned my itinerary for the next day. I had to find out what had happened to Gwen Larkin.

I was still in the chapel when the nuns arrived for evening prayers. I left with them, walking slowly back to the Mother House for dinner. There are curious rituals in a convent. In this one as in mine, each nun had her own little drawer in the community room where she kept her napkin ring and her mug. On weekdays her mail would be left in that drawer. As a guest, I had no drawer, but I had thought to bring along a mug for my coffee as I had brought my own towels, sheets, and soap. The mug was handy after dinner when we sat in front of the TV and drank coffee. The program of choice that evening was "60 Minutes," after which the nuns left to shower and get ready for bed. In a convent with younger nuns, the older ones may leave first, but there were no younger nuns here, and by eight o'clock they had all been awake for fifteen hours. Some of them had slipped away during the program to get to bed early.

I was about to leave myself when a nun I didn't know came into the room and called me. "You're wanted on the phone," she said.

I followed her to the phone in the foyer.

"Miss Bennett?" a man's voice said.

"Yes, it is."

"This is Ken Parker at Steuben Press. I've done some calling around about J.J. Eberling."

"Yes," I said eagerly.

"I can't give you specifics and I probably shouldn't say anything at all, but I heard a couple of things. It's all rumor and speculation, you understand, and I can't say too much because I don't want to get my pants sued off me, but the word is, there was a payoff."

"J.J. Eberling paid someone off?"

"That's about all I can tell you. You were right when you said people were beholden. That's the absolutely right-on-the-target word for it. I don't know how you'll crack it, but keep me out of it, OK? Good night, Miss Bennett."

He hung up before I could return his farewell. A payoff. To whom? And why? The only money I knew about was the thousand dollars J.J. had given to Joanne Beadles, and Joanne had given to her mother. Was that the payoff he was talking about? What could a nineteen-year-old girl have known or done to warrant a payoff? Had there been more—paid to other people? I hoped Jack would be able to find her—if she was still alive.

And for yet another time I wondered if I was chasing the wrong man.

21

Carol Stifler's list reflected her penchant for organization. Next to each death there was a date, or an approximate date. And next to each new address was the date of the move. So I knew where Fred Larkin had lived and when he had moved to each new address. He had lived in his current house for twenty years, and I guessed that he had lived there with his current wife. That left two addresses that covered ten years, and both of them were in the central part of the state. That gave me the start of my Monday morning itinerary. I would start west and work my way east, eventually getting home by evening. Tuesday morning I had a class to teach.

By nine A.M. I was in the county building of the nearer address. It was the second one Larkin had lived in, but it made sense to start close. Since I had a time frame, my search was limited to the years he had lived there. I found a sympathetic young woman who got me started. I went through all the recorded divorces in the eight-year period Fred Larkin had lived in the county. There was no mention of his name.

Then I tried the deaths. Plenty of people had died in those eight years, but none of them was Gwendolyn Larkin. I got in my car and drove east.

At my second stop, the county seat in the Larkins' first post-Studsburg home, I had only two years of records to scan. There was no divorce here either, and I moved on to the deaths. It didn't take long to find what I was looking for. Less than a year after leaving Studsburg, Mrs. Gwendolyn

Larkin had died an accidental death. I wrote down the date and then found the sheriff's office.

It wasn't the first time I had tried to get hold of old police records, and it wasn't the first time I was given a runaround. No one wants to go looking in dusty old files, and I couldn't hang around all day waiting for someone to find time to do me a favor. I finally persuaded someone that Mrs. Larkin was a very important person to me and I needed to know how she had died. He looked at his watch meaningfully before he agreed to go down to the basement to look up the file on her death.

I was getting hungry myself at that point, but I didn't want to give up if there was a chance I could learn something. I knew that in a pinch Jack could get me the information, but it might take time, and although all the important events had happened decades ago, I felt pressed to learn as much as I could as fast as I could, as though I were working against some deadline that was rapidly closing in on me.

The officer was gone quite a while, and I sat part of the time and walked around part of the time, hoping he hadn't ducked out on me.

He hadn't. He finally came through the door with a file folder in his hand. I stood up and walked to the counter while he took his place behind it.

"Gwendolyn Larkin, husband Fred?" he said.

"That's it."

"Car accident."

"Was anyone else hurt?"

"Only one vehicle involved. No one else in her car."

"How did it happen?"

"It was winter, icy stretch, car went off the road, hit a tree."

"And they're sure no one else was in the car with her?"

"Ma'am," he said with unctuous politeness, "in an accidental death there's an investigation. Also an autopsy. Mrs. Larkin was at the wheel. It was twenty-nine years ago and she wasn't wearing a seat belt. Given the details in the accident report—road conditions, auto damage, speed—I'd estimate it didn't take her more than a couple of seconds to die after the car made contact.''

''Thank you.''

''Can I have my lunch now?''

I got a sandwich near the courthouse and then drove east. I wasn't sure where I was going. I knew I had to confront Fred Larkin with Candy Phillips, and there was enough time today to do that. Eventually I would have to drive into Pennsylvania and see if I could find the place that Candy's letters were forwarded to, but it was much too late to think about that today. Then I remembered Amy Broderick's brother, Jerry Mulholland.

I had sort of been waiting to call him from home. Now I decided to try his office number instead of waiting for tonight. I pulled into a gas station, filled the tank, and used their pay phone.

''Mulholland,'' a voice answered.

I told him who I was.

''Oh yeah. Amy said you'd be calling. Want to stir up old memories, I hear.''

''I hope they're still good and sharp. I'm interested in what you remember about your eighth grade teacher.''

''You mean the delectable Miss Phillips.''

I smiled. He sounded like a nice guy and he didn't mind being called. ''Tell me what you remember.''

''God, she was something. She got hormones flowing I didn't even know I had. I was thirteen or fourteen and she had to be ten years older, but I was willing to do anything to make it work. But I had a lot of competition from the other guys in my class. Everyone was in love with her. She was really cute. And a good teacher, by the way.''

''Any competition from adult males?''

''Yeah, there was that, too.''

''You remember seeing her with anyone special?''

''You looking for a scandal? Could be. She was parked

one night with Mayor Larkin. I really didn't get it. He must've been forty, and he didn't have half my personality.''

I could believe it. "You saw them together in a car?'' I hoped I didn't sound as elated as I felt.

"Yeah. His car. Down by the athletic field one night when there wasn't any game on.''

"Were they . . . I mean . . . ?''

"Necking? Not when I saw them. They were just talking, planning her life without me. Boy, did I have the hots for her.''

"You sound like a very honest man, Mr. Mulholland. Did you tell your parents about it?''

"Nah. I was nuts about her. I didn't want to get her in trouble. I was with a couple of friends that night. We decided to keep it to ourselves. Call me Jerry, OK?''

"Was that the only time it happened?''

"Other guys saw her with him other times. It was always in his car. She had this old VW he probably couldn't fit in.''

"Any possibility that someone in your parents' generation saw them together?''

"Every possibility. It was a small town. Anywhere you went, someone could drive by or walk by with his dog. One of my friends saw them once at the top of the hill. Not where the farm was, the other side of town. Near those people—what the hell was their name? Funny name, German-sounding.''

"Could it have been Degenkamp?''

"Degenkamp, right. My friend lived near the Degenkamps. He saw them drive by.''

"You've really been very helpful, Jerry.''

"Call any time. You want to tell me why you're asking? Amy didn't say.''

I had a pang of guilt. Even after so long, he wouldn't take my message with equanimity, and I hated to be the one to tell him. "Can I pass until I'm sure?''

"If you promise to call.''

"I will.'' It wouldn't be the best day of my life.

* * *

Fred Larkin wasn't waiting at the door for me this time. In fact, he wasn't at home, but his wife was. She recognized me and invited me in. Her husband had gone into town a little while ago and should be back soon, she told me. In the meantime, how would I like a cup of coffee? I said I'd like that very much.

We sat in her large kitchen outfitted with handsome cabinets and good-looking appliances. I remarked that she must enjoy cooking, and she said she did. As if to prove her skills, she brought out some home-baked cookies and put them on the table.

"I was going to ask you about Studsburg," I said after complimenting her on the cookies, "but I realized just this morning that you hadn't lived there."

She studied me before answering. She was an extremely attractive woman, even younger than I had first judged. She was quite tall and graceful, her hands well manicured, her hair thick and cut short, falling in place naturally. I didn't think she spent much time at the hairdresser, and probably looked better than most of the women who did. At home in her own kitchen, she was wearing a suede vest over a silk blouse, and dark brown wool pants over glossy brown boots.

"I met Fred after his first wife died in a tragic accident," she said.

"What happened?"

"She lost control of her car one night. When the police found the car, she was already dead. Fred was devastated. They'd known each other since they were children."

I was about to say something when the front door opened and Fred Larkin called a cheery hello to his wife.

"In the kitchen, dear. We have company."

He would know that, of course. My car was parked outside. In the country you can't hide by parking around the corner.

"Well, Miss Bennett. What brings you here?"

"A couple of questions. I won't trouble you for long. I have to be getting back."

"Where is it you get back to?"

"I live near New York."

"Long trip to ask a few questions."

"I had some other business in the area." I got up from the table and thanked his wife for the coffee.

"I'm kind of busy myself, so let's see if we can make it pretty quick." His expansive charm of last Thursday had been replaced with a petulance I found intimidating. He walked into the family room with its trophies and photos, and I followed.

"I wonder if you would tell me about Candida Phillips," I said.

He was smart enough not to dodge. On Thursday he had spun a fable for me, a pretty story told by an all-knowing adult to a wide-eyed child. It had had all the elements of a fairy tale: good people grew up together and lived happy lives; everyone was friendly, and the rich helped the poor; men and women met as children, grew up, and married each other, living happily ever after; the mayor attended baptisms and weddings and gave presents on all occasions, and *they kept Mr. Dietrich on even though the classes shrank down to almost nothing.* But the name Candida Phillips told him I hadn't bought it, and what was worse, someone may have cracked and told me things that had been buried for thirty years.

He gave me a tight little smile. "Now, that's a name I haven't heard since I left Studsburg. Yes, there was a Miss Phillips that last year. She taught in the school. Came from nowhere, and went back to nowhere."

"I believe you interviewed her for the job."

He knit his heavy white eyebrows together. Was he wondering if Henry Degenkamp was the source? "I suppose I did. As mayor, I had a lot of diverse duties. It fell to me to notify a family when a mishap occurred to their son and to administer punishment when a Halloween prank got out of hand. Yes, I interviewed Miss Phillips, as I interviewed the janitor who came in and cleaned the school twice a week.''

"Do you know where she went at the end of the school year?''

"I suppose to another school somewhere. She was a teacher, after all. Teachers teach in schools." His voice had gotten a hard edge, a derisive nastiness that good people like the Stiflers and Mulhollands had surely never heard.

"If you interviewed her, you must have written her a reference." I had seen it in the file along with one written by Scofield.

"I might have. These aren't the things I can pull out of my memory. What I remember is the town, how it felt, how people treated each other." He glanced at the aerial photograph, the proof that heaven had once existed on earth.

"I'm a little surprised you didn't remember her when we spoke a couple of days ago. She spent a whole year in Studsburg, and a number of people saw you with her. In the evening," I added.

He kept himself in check, but I sensed the anger below the good-old-boy surface. "You are now getting personal and you are putting me in the awkward position of having to say things about someone who is not here to defend herself. Miss Phillips was a new, young teacher—Studsburg may have been her first assignment, I don't recall—and young people in every profession need guidance. That was another task that fell to me that year, helping out a young teacher."

"Can you tell me what her problem was, Mr. Larkin?"

"It isn't any of your business, Miss Bennett, but young women sometimes become involved with the wrong men. Whether it's their fault or not makes no difference. Families are sacred. Studsburg was an old-fashioned, family-centered town. I saw to it that it remained that way right to the end."

It was interesting that he had glided from professional assistance to family guidance. "Do you always give guidance to young women in your car?"

"Young woman, you are very close to being thrown out

of this house. I shouldn't honor that snide question with an answer, but I'll tell you this much: My office was in my home. I had something personal and delicate to discuss with Miss Phillips, and I considered it better to meet her where no one would be aware that she was being chastised. If someone saw us together and chose to draw a foolish conclusion, well, I can't be responsible for people's stupidity or malicious intentions. I had her best interests at heart, you may believe me."

"Did you ever see Candy Phillips after the last day of school?" I asked.

He looked me in the eye. "I never did," he said. "And now I think it's time for you to go."

I went out to my car feeling high as a kite. He had never once asked why I was interested in Candy Phillips. He didn't have to. He knew.

22

It was still reasonably early when I saw the towers of Cornell rising above Cayuga Lake. It's all uphill to the campus and the little villages adjacent to it. I needed only one stop to inquire for directions to reach the Degenkamps' house. This time a man opened the front door. He was Eric Degenkamp, a middle-aged version of his father, dressed in dark corduroy pants, a sporty shirt, and a sweater that may have been cashmere.

"What's going on here?" he asked when I told him who I was.

"I don't know what you mean. I want to talk to your father and mother."

"My father isn't here and—"

"Who's there, Eric?" Ellie Degenkamp called from inside in a shrill voice. "Is your dad back yet?"

"Not yet, Mom."

"Did he get a phone call?" I asked.

"About an hour ago. Did you call him?"

"No, but I think I know who did."

Ellie was standing behind her son, looking frightened to death. "You," she said accusingly. "You better tell me what's going on and where Henry is."

"I left Fred Larkin an hour ago, Mrs. Degenkamp. I was talking to him about Candy Phillips. That's all I know."

"Candy Phillips," she said angrily. "Can't you leave well enough alone?"

"Maybe you can tell me about her," I said gently.

"Tell you what? She was a little slut that they brought in to teach the last year of Studsburg. God knows what damage she did to those children."

"The children loved her."

"You've talked to the children?"

"Some of them."

"What do twelve-year-olds know?"

"I think they're a pretty good judge of character."

"She didn't have any character to judge." Ellie was angry and forthright, the superficial sweetness that she normally turned on the world dissolved in anger and worry and a touch of bitterness. "What did Fred tell you?"

"That she taught in Studsburg one year. That she came from nowhere and went to nowhere. Not much else."

"Well, you won't get anything out of me, because there isn't anything else. But I want to know where Henry is. It looks like snow out there and he shouldn't be driving."

"Why don't you call Fred Larkin?" I said.

We had all been standing just inside the front door. Now

Ellie went into the kitchen to make her phone call while Eric and I went to the living room.

A few minutes later she joined us, flopping into a chair, her short white hair lifting and falling as she sat. Her son went and knelt beside her. "Dad isn't there," she said, her voice cracking. "Fred called just after Miss Bennett left. He didn't ask him to come, he just said Miss Bennett might be on her way."

"Maybe he didn't want to talk to her, Mom," Eric said. "Maybe he just went out to have a cup of coffee."

"That's not like Henry." She shook her head. Then she looked up at me. "Why are you doing this?" she wailed.

"Mrs. Degenkamp, were Fred Larkin and Candy Phillips lovers that year?"

"I don't know," she said weakly. "I don't know anything anymore. He said they weren't."

"Did you believe him?"

She thought about it. "I thought he and . . . he and his wife were happy."

"Why did you call her a slut?"

"Please go away," she said. "Eric, go and look for him. Maybe he's reading the papers at the library. Or having coffee at that new place."

Eric patted her shoulder and got up to go. I wrote my name and phone number on a slip of paper and gave it to her.

"I'll be at this number tonight. Will you call me and let me know what happened to him?"

She nodded. I followed Eric to the door. Ellie's forecast had been accurate. Huge snowflakes were falling. Although the street was clear, the lawns were turning white. I wondered if this would be the end of the drought, if Studsburg was about to sink into a lake of oblivion again. I had a desperate urge to know the truth before Candy Phillips's grave was underwater for the second time.

Outside the house, Eric zipped up a heavy jacket and pulled a knitted cap on his head. The snow was coming down furiously.

"Would you like to tell me what's going on?" he said.

"A woman was murdered in Studsburg, probably on the Fourth of July thirty years ago, the last day of the town's existence. Were you there that day?"

"No. And I wasn't there any part of that year."

"I'm trying to find out who she was and why she was killed."

"That sounds like a police matter to me. Why don't you leave it to them?"

"Has anyone from the sheriff's office been here to question your parents?"

"No one."

"That's why I can't leave it to them. They're not trying very hard. When the body was found, there was a media circus for a day or two. Now that the cameras are gone, no one really cares very much."

"I can assure you my parents had nothing to do with anyone's death."

"I agree with you." I wasn't all that sure, but I decided it was better to sound sure if there was any chance he might cooperate with me. "But they know something they don't want to talk about. I'm sure you see that. And your father was obviously very disturbed when Fred Larkin called. Someone's going to tell me eventually."

"I'll talk to my mother when I get back. Maybe she's protecting someone."

"Thank you. I hope you find your father."

"I'm sure I will." But he didn't look sure. He looked very worried.

It was one of those snows that had dedicated itself to a small geographical area. Before I reached Binghamton I was out of it, and although the sky never cleared, I made it home without trouble.

I went through the letters that had piled up inside my front door without opening any of them. Nothing looked important or urgent. Instead, I called St. Stephen's and made an appointment to see Sister Joseph after tomorrow's class.

As I hung up, Carol Stifler called. I didn't tell her what I had learned about Gwen Larkin, but I asked her if she kept any of the Christmas cards Fred Larkin sent every year.

"All of them," she said. "They always have a sketch or photo of Studsburg on the front. You want to see them?"

"If you wouldn't mind."

"Come on over. We'd rather talk to you than watch TV any time."

Before leaving, I called the Degenkamps' number. It was answered by a harried-sounding Eric.

"This is Chris Bennett. Have you found him?"

"No, and my mother's a wreck. We all are. We've called the police, and they found his car a little while ago."

"Where?"

"Several blocks from here, a mile maybe. We've been up and down the streets for hours, but there's no sign of him. The police think he got disoriented, but that never happened to my father before. Wait a minute. My mother wants to talk to you."

"Christine?"

"Yes, Mrs. Degenkamp."

"I want you to know that I don't know anything about that body they found in the church basement, and neither does Henry. I couldn't tell you what Fred Larkin knows, but I don't think he knows anything either. But you asked us last week about the newspaper, the last one J.J. printed. We never got it." Her voice was so controlled, I had the feeling she had taken something to calm herself down.

"Do you know why? Did you ask?"

"It's because Fred Larkin didn't want them given out. We saw the fight. That's the one thing we didn't tell you."

"What fight?"

"Fred and J.J. We were coming down Main Street to say our good-byes and pick up our *Herald*—J.J. had promised we'd all be in it—and they were both right there at the bridge, Fred in a real frenzy. I thought they might come to blows.''

"Did you hear anything they said?'' I asked.

"Couldn't hear a word. After Fred left, J.J. waved us on, said there weren't any papers left, which you could see was a lie because he had them piled right there next to him. He just wouldn't give them out.''

"Did you ever ask either one of them about it, Mrs. Degenkamp?''

"We asked Fred next time we saw him, which was a couple of months later. He said he couldn't betray a trust. That's just how he put it, he couldn't betray a trust. That was all he would say.''

"Do you think it had something to do with his wife?'' I asked.

"I couldn't say.''

"She died not long after that.''

"That was a real tragedy, a young, beautiful woman like that.''

"Mrs. Degenkamp, when I asked you today if Fred Larkin and Candy Phillips were lovers, you said Fred said they weren't. You asked him about it.''

"Well, something was going on. They were meeting together. Some youngsters saw them down in the park together, and Henry saw them one night. Someone else saw them in another town once. Fred said she was in trouble and needed help.''

"Did you believe him?''

"Why shouldn't I?''

I couldn't think of any reason offhand why she shouldn't. "I appreciate your—'' I began when she interrupted me.

"It's the police,'' she said. "I think they've found Henry.'' She hung up the phone with a clatter, and that was the end of our conversation.

By the time I got to the Stiflers', I was on my personal reserve tank of energy. Carol had a shoe box ready, full of Christmas cards she hadn't had the heart to throw out. There were enough from Fred Larkin to account for three decades of Christmases past.

They were oversize and very handsome. The oldest one, dating back almost thirty years, had the aerial photo on the front. Later ones had photos of St. Mary Immaculate, the Main Street bridge, the school, the Simpsons' farm, and sketches of houses, the trout stream, the general store, and other recognizable places in town. Inside, every card was identical. All were printed: "Merry Christmas to all our friends. Mayor Fred Larkin and Family." No one ever put pen to paper to write a personal note.

I put them back in the box. "Gwen Larkin was killed in an automobile accident almost thirty years ago," I said.

They looked at me as though I had declared Fred himself had died.

"Are you sure?" Carol said finally.

"I saw the death certificate this morning. I talked to his second wife about it."

"You mean he's been hiding her death?" Harry said.

"At least from the Studsburg people. The Degenkamps know, but I suspect they've been personal friends. Tell me, did you invite the Larkins to Richard's baptism?"

"We sent him an invitation," Carol said. "He was on Harry's mother's list. He wrote back that he couldn't make it."

But he could have been in the church that afternoon, digging out Candy's body to retrieve a lost miraculous medal. "Did either of you know Candy Phillips, the teacher they hired for the last year?"

They looked at each other and shook their heads.

"Did you ever hear that Fred Larkin was involved with another woman?"

"Fred?" Harry said. "Sounds a little crazy. He married Gwen Harvey when he came back from college. The Harveys lived in Studsburg, and Gwen was an exceptionally beautiful woman. I suppose she was about my mother's age, but even as a kid, I recognized that she was very beautiful. Everybody knew they'd known each other since school days. They had a son a couple of years younger than me, and they sure as hell looked like a happy couple." He got up. "This is just nuts." He went to the kitchen and made a phone call.

While he was gone, I went through the *Herald* again. Gwen Larkin, in her early forties, was as beautiful as everyone said. Fred was pretty good-looking himself. In the eighth grade they must have been a cute young couple. In one large formal picture, Fred and Gwen were surrounded by other important Studsburg personages. Father Hartman was there, and so was Irwin Kaufman, who had been on the committee that interviewed Candy.

Harry came back. "I just talked to my mother." He looked less than happy. "It took some prodding, but she laid it out for me eventually. She knew who the Phillips woman was and she knew there was talk about her and Fred Larkin. She didn't want it spread around, which is why she needed prodding. Then I asked her about Gwen Larkin. She never knew Gwen was dead."

Jack had spent the better part of the day researching Joanne Beadles for me. She had definitely occupied the apartment that the security check had been sent to, and he had traced her to another apartment in Manhattan she had apparently occupied for a long time. In New York in the sixties you could probably still find yourself a rent-controlled apartment at a good price—even if you had to make a payoff to an intermediary for the privilege of occupying it—and once you were in it, anywhere else you moved would cost an arm and a leg by comparison.

"I need more time," he said. "But it doesn't look like anyone killed her thirty years ago."

I was relieved to hear that. "Anything on gun ownership?" I asked.

"Got a partial answer there. I called Albany to have someone check the records for the names you gave me. They've got a bunch of civilians working up there now, and they don't hop to it when they get a request the way the guys on the job do. So it'll be a couple of days till I get an answer. But I got an idea while I was driving home, and it panned out. It occurred to me one of those guys, the rich one you said had been an army brat, might have been a collector. For that you need a federal license, not a state one, and the feds give you a quick answer. They did and he was.''

''J.J. collected guns?''

''Everything from a couple of Civil War handguns to some World War One babies I'd guess his daddy brought home and some he probably pocketed himself in World War Two. Also a few more modern revolvers.''

''Jack, give me the bottom line.''

''You mean did he own a thirty-eight that could have killed your schoolteacher? More than one.''

''Wow.''

He asked if I'd learned anything, and I told him I was too tired to think. It was the understatement of the day.

23

The class I teach each Tuesday morning is kind of a lifeline. At thirty I find myself out of touch with people ten or twelve years younger than I. The neighbors with whom I have formed friendships are my age or older. All of them are married, homeowners, parents, and profess to be concerned citizens. Their interests range from cinch bugs to disposable diapers, with a strong emphasis on local politics.

My students, on the other hand, are all single, striving, female, and intellectually sharp. Most of them are more sexually experienced than I and more casual—or perhaps comfortable—with their sexuality. As human beings they represent the same range of personalities I had been teaching at St. Stephen's College. There are the painfully shy, quiet ones who write magnificent papers, the loud, opinionated ones, some of whom write well and some of whom are all hot air. One girl invariably falls asleep about ten-thirty in the morning, leaving me to wonder whether she works all night or just finds the class boring. I have to admit that the latter possibility gives me my weekly dose of humility.

On that Tuesday I found myself revived and invigorated by my students. Together we had drawn up the question: I am a nineties woman. This poetry was written more than two centuries ago. Why should I bother?

At least one person thought she shouldn't. The rest produced generally interesting arguments, documented with poems we had been discussing, on why they should. Even my sleeper contributed a few thoughts before retiring into dreamland.

I left the college feeling remarkably refreshed and took off for St. Stephen's, which lies not far from the Hudson well along the way to Albany. There was evidence of recent snow, and I wondered if Ithaca's weather had moved east during the night. My arrival occasioned smiles and hugs from people who had functioned for many years as my family. I had the sense of coming home.

Joseph, my friend, former spiritual director, and present General Superior, was called while I was chatting with brown-habited nuns, and she came down to greet me and separate me from them. We went upstairs to the large room that was her office, study, and conference room, a place that has barely changed in the fifteen years since I first saw it.

Our lunch was on two separate trays on the long table, a thermos pitcher of coffee near one tray. As I spotted the pitcher, it occurred to me that the Superior of the Sacred Heart Convent could use one. I had seen her carrying a mug to the kitchen to replenish it, a long walk from her study, and

I thought she would surely appreciate having a source of hot coffee nearby.

"You're looking well," Joseph said as we sat down. "Perhaps a little thinner than last time. I hope you aren't planning to model for a fashion magazine."

"Not in this lifetime. I just haven't thought much about meals since I started looking into this murder."

"He isn't likely to kill again, Chris, even if it takes you an extra day to find him."

"Someone's already been hurt by this," I said, thinking I should try to call the Degenkamps and see how Henry was doing.

"Start from some reasonable place, geographical or chronological, and tell me what I need to know." Joseph poured coffee for both of us, and I took out the steno book that I used to take notes.

I started with geography. On a sheet of typing paper that I found on the table, I sketched the Studsburg that I had seen on Fred Larkin's aerial photo and that I had visited. At the front left center was St. Mary Immaculate, the focal point of the town. Off to the right was the Simpsons' farm. Toward the top of the horizontal sheet, still to the right, was where the Degenkamps and Stiflers had lived. Moving downhill, which was left, I drew in Main Street and the bridge. Then I filled in the wooded area and the park or athletic field, both on the left side of the town. I realized I had no sense of direction, where north was, for instance, but it didn't seem important. When I was finished, I turned it around so it faced Joseph.

Then I explained my identification of Candida Phillips from the records in the county building and the meeting with the Thurstons, mother and daughter. I told her how almost everyone in the town had conveniently forgotten the existence of Candy, even those who had interviewed her for the job of teacher, except for one woman, Mrs. Mulholland, who admitted later to her daughter she was sorry she had mentioned her. There was Fred Larkin, the mayor of Studsburg, and his wife, Gwen, who had died in an accident that I considered suspicious, or at the very least mysterious, and whose death had been kept a secret for all these years except to those closest to Larkin. There was Henry Degenkamp, who knew something was going on but wouldn't talk about it. But the children, now grown, had talked, linking Candy to the mayor.

"What did the mayor say to that?" Joseph asked. "I assume you told him."

"I did. He was a little slippery when he answered me. He started out saying he had to give her professional help and finished by saying he had given her 'family guidance,' that she had become involved with a man who wasn't appropriate."

Joseph smiled. "A nice way to tell the truth if he was the man."

"But he may not have been." That led me to J.J. Eberling, army brat, well off, syndicated columnist, publisher of the *Studsburg Herald*, abuser of one teenage girl and possibly another, and owner of more than one .38 revolver.

"But I have something that rules him out as a killer," I said, opening my purse and fishing out the miraculous medal. I put it on the table near Joseph's lunch tray. "Whoever opened the grave two and a half weeks ago found this inside and dropped it in his hurry to get away. I heard it fall. J.J. Eberling has been dead for years and he wasn't a Catholic. But the mayor is a Catholic, and his mother might have been born in 1898. I still haven't found out what her name was. He was invited to the baptism I went to, but he declined, probably because he never told most of the guests that his wife had died twenty-nine years ago. But that doesn't mean he didn't come to the church that afternoon and dig open the grave."

"Certainly a possibility," Joseph said. She had moved her lunch tray aside and now sat with her hands folded in front of her on the table. Her face showed nothing, but her eyes seemed to be concentrating, as though it were the eyes that heard the story.

"And then there's poor Henry Degenkamp. He knew Candy, he knew the rumors about her and the mayor. He was at the baptism two weeks ago. But he's well into his eighties. I don't think he could have moved that stone without some help, and the medal couldn't be his or his mother's. The dates are wrong."

"Entirely wrong," Joseph agreed.

"I asked Father Hartman if anyone fitted the date and initials, but he couldn't think of anyone."

"Is that it then?"

"Not completely." I told her then about the publisher of the Steuben Press and his brief message—there was a payoff—and about the money Joanne Beadles gave her mother. And then I finished with the last issue of the *Studsburg Herald*.

"So something in that paper may indicate who the killer is if one can just figure out how to interpret it." She picked up the medal, looking at it carefully for the first time. "It's not unusual. There must be hundreds like it. I think my niece has the same one." She laid it squarely on my sketch of St. Mary Immaculate.

"But the killer must have felt it would identify him."

"How could it identify him if it was sealed in a grave?"

"Suppose it became unsealed," I said. "Suppose the state came in and said the church was in danger of collapsing and should be bulldozed the way all the other buildings in Studsburg were."

"But they didn't," Joseph said. "They said exactly the opposite. They declared the church structurally safe. That's why your friend's baby was baptized there."

"True."

"No, I think there's a possibility you haven't considered, and Studsburg being the kind of town it was, you have to consider it. This was a town protecting its own and guarding some kind of secret. If it's a money secret and J.J. Eberling was involved, Candy may have found out about it, and it may have cost her her life. But then why did J.J. Eberling publish a paper that gave the secret of her death away? If anyone knew what was in that paper, he did. So perhaps it was love, and the town closed ranks to protect her lover because he was respected.''

"It was more than respect, Joseph. They were beholden to both J.J. and the mayor. Everyone seemed to be the beneficiary of their kindness.''

"That makes sense,'' Joseph said. "It stretches credulity to believe that even half the population of that town, say two hundred people, could keep silent about a murder for thirty years. Someone would have broken his silence; someone's conscience would have gotten the better of him. I think the town didn't know there'd been a murder till you discovered it. They knew something else, and the something else is what they've been trying to keep you from learning. In fact''—she looked away from the table—''there may have been more than one secret. From what you've told me about them, I would almost guess that J.J. Eberling and the mayor didn't especially like each other. There may have been a quiet battle for power between them, each of them seeing himself as the leader of that little village. But in the end, they needed each other just the way the whole town needed them.''

"A kind of mutual blackmail,'' I said.

"It's possible, isn't it? It reminds me of the search for the cause of a deadly disease. Sometimes there are many causes. And sometimes,'' she said thoughtfully, "what looks like one disease is really many diseases.''

"But Candy Phillips's killer is still alive, whichever disease she was part of.''

"Perhaps,'' Joseph said, "and perhaps not. You see, the person who opened that grave in the church may not have been a killer revisiting the scene of his crime. It could have been someone who had heard about the murder, and he—or she—wanted to know the truth. Perhaps he leaned over the remains and his chain caught on the stone and broke. How clean was the floor that night?''

It struck me as she asked the question that I should have seen it myself. The basement was three-quarters below ground level and the floor had been slick and silty, not like the upstairs floor, which had been carefully cleaned for the baptism. I had even noticed when I returned a week later that it was cleaner than when I first saw it, ostensibly because the police had been looking for leads.

"It was dirty," I said. "I couldn't have heard the medal fall, because it wouldn't have made a sound on the floor. You're right. He bent down and the medal hit the rock or the chain caught and broke, and the medal bounced on the stone before it hit the floor. And you know, it should have been much dirtier, Joseph, if it spent thirty years in dirty water. The skeleton was covered with mud."

"I think the suggestion of a payoff was a sound one. I don't know if it will lead you to a killer, but it should answer a lot of questions."

"Thank you, Joseph."

She pushed the map across the table to me, and I picked up the medal, rubbed it between my fingers, and put it back in my purse.

As I got up from the table, she said, "Take the map, too. I think you need it more than I."

24

The first thing I did when I got home was to call the Degenkamps. The younger Mrs. Degenkamp answered.

"I'm afraid the news is bad," she said. "My father-in-law was found lying on the ground in a wooded area about a mile from here. He was unconscious and he died before they could get him to a hospital."

I must have made a sound. I know that I felt a wave of shock and a total inability to speak.

"It was very shocking to us, too," she said. "I don't know what happened to upset him yesterday."

"He got a phone call," I said. "From Fred Larkin."

"Whatever it was, he picked up and left a little while later, and they didn't find him for hours."

"Do they know what he died of?"

"They think a heart attack or exposure or perhaps a combination of both. Because of the circumstances, there has to be an autopsy. We should know more tomorrow."

"I'm very sorry, Mrs. Degenkamp. I hope you'll convey my sympathy to your mother-in-law."

"I'll have to wait till she's more composed. This has hit her like a ton of bricks."

"Have you scheduled the funeral?"

"Friday, if they release the body in time."

I said a few more inadequate words and hung up. Old Henry Degenkamp had seen something or knew something. Now it was lost along with his life. What had Fred Larkin said to him? It had to be more than the possibility of my arrival. I had already spoken to the Degenkamps last week, and they had effectively put me off. Had Larkin threatened him?

I boiled water and made a cup of tea. I'm not much of a cook, but I brew tea with care. Even inhaling its fumes on a cold day makes me feel good. With the cup beside me, I called Jack at the Sixty-fifth Precinct in Brooklyn. He was actually there.

"Hey, good to hear from you. How's things?"

I told him about Henry Degenkamp.

"Chris, honey, get in your car and drive down to Brooklyn. It's crazy for you to be alone, and I've got things to tell you. We'll have dinner after my class. I'll cook, I'll listen, and I'll keep you warm and happy all night."

"You're a sweetheart," I said.

"I know. My sister told me last time I talked to her. How about it?"

"I'm on my way."

I don't consider myself an expert in man-woman relationships, contemporary or otherwise. But if I were to offer one piece of advice to a woman in search of the man she would like to love, it would be to find one who enjoys cooking. I know I place myself hopelessly outside the mainstream when I say I find cooking a chore, but I got along for thirty years without having to feed myself—with the exception of one year of graduate study when I had my own tiny apartment—and my current efforts are geared toward keeping me alive, not toward achieving taste sensations.

Jack, on the other hand, has lived by himself for several years, and he enjoys food the way some people enjoy music and art. What's more, his sister is part owner of a fledgling catering service, so he is frequently the beneficiary of enticing samples and leftovers, the tastes of which inspire him to greater culinary activities, and me to shrink from the work and talent I'm sure are involved in preparing such attractive and wonderful foods.

On that evening he had a foil container of a fabulous chicken concoction made with unpronounceable mushrooms. He cooked rice and whipped up a salad while I cut grapefruit for us to start with.

"We're a good team," he said, looking in the oven, where the chicken was warming, to check I could not imagine what.

"You cook the food and I cut the grapefruit. If that's all it takes to play on your team, I'll sign up for the season."

"And I'll have you out of the grapefruit league in no time. I'm leaving you the dishes, pots, and pans. Is that even enough?"

"Does that mean I get to throw away the foil container?"

"You get to do that, too. Right."

He has the sweetest smile I've ever seen on a man. When it comes my way, I have trouble remembering how tough and determined he can look when he finds himself in a danger zone.

The first taste of that chicken put me in rapture. ''It's better than good,'' I said. ''Tell your sister the Sacred Heart Convent never ate like this.''

''How could they afford it? Those mushrooms are ten bucks a pound.''

''Maybe when this is over I'll bring the nuns a dinner's worth.''

''My sister'll donate it. How's that?''

''I'll do the donating. Jack, tell me about Joanne Beadles.''

''I found her.''

''You did?''

''You didn't think I lured you here under false pretenses?''

''Oh, that's wonderful. Tell me about it.''

''Eat first. Talk afterward.''

Over coffee and a luscious chocolate cake, he told me. He had started by going to the building where Joanne Beadles had first lived when she came to New York thirty years ago. It was an old building in the West Forties, happily not one of many that had been torn down for a new high-rise. The super was in his sixties and had been running the building since shortly before Joanne moved in. He remembered her because she was young and most of his tenants were older, because she paid the first month's rent and the security in cash from what looked like a thick roll of bills, and because there was a strange incident several months after she moved in. Someone had beaten her up, and she asked the super to get her an ambulance.

''Do you think she was a prostitute?'' I asked.

''The guy doesn't think so. He never saw men come and go, and nothing like that ever happened again.''

''Did she identify the man?''

''Doesn't look that way. There's no record of the case. I checked the precinct files. The files for that year are already on microfiche, so I didn't have to spend half a year looking through paper records.''

According to the super's books, Joanne had stayed in the apartment for about three years. He had had the feeling that she was an actress, but he didn't know what made him think that. In any case, she moved out one day, having given proper notice, and he never saw her again.

Jack has a unique way of taking notes which is peculiarly his own. He starts with a clean sheet of white, unlined paper, which he folds in half horizontally. He then starts writing on it, sometimes along a short edge, sometimes hit or miss. At some point he decides the subject matter warrants a clean surface and he folds the paper in half again, clean side out, and resumes writing. His notes end up looking haphazard if you flatten out the sheet, which of course, he never does. His system of information retrieval is strictly intuitive. He folds and unfolds, turns and turns again. But he always seems to come up with what he's looking for. As he related his search, he referred to one of his wonderful note sheets, and I marveled for the hundredth time at his system.

When Joanne left the apartment, she left no forwarding address, at least not with the super. So Jack went to the main post office on Eighth Avenue across from Madison Square Garden. I was somewhat amused at the parallel courses our investigations had taken. In my search for Candy Phillips's whereabouts I had visited her home and subsequently gone to the post office, albeit a much smaller one. In Jack's case he had eventually found what he was looking for with the help of the Postal Inspector's office. It's amazing how many old records can be found if you know where to look. Joanne Beadles had moved up to the West Eighties and changed her name at the same time. She had married Lawrence Knox.

"And believe it or not, she's still there."

"She only moved once in thirty years?"

"In New York, you get a good apartment, it doesn't pay to give it up. You end up paying more for less. Nowadays who gets the apartment is part of the divorce settlement."

"This is just great, Jack."

"And if you look in the phone book, the greatest source of names, addresses, and phone numbers ever compiled, you'll find Lawrence Knox right there."

"I can't believe it. I thought she would have gone to California or something and I'd never find her."

"Hey, we love to hate it, but New York's a great place to live." We had finished our cake and coffee by then, and he had his arm around me. I let my head slide down to his shoulder and put my arms around him.

He said, "Mm," and kissed the side of my face.

"I have dishes to do," I said.

"It's my house, I do the dishes."

"I thought we were a team."

"You really go by the book, don't you?"

I said, "Mm," and kissed his neck.

"Tell you what. We'll do them together and then we'll do something else together."

"Sounds good to me."

It was.

25

One thing I don't do is call before I come. In this case especially, I didn't know what Joanne née Beadles would be willing to talk about and what might put her off so strongly that she might refuse to speak to me at all. Jack was on his usual ten-to-six schedule, so we got up about eight and had breakfast together.

"You look better already," he said at the breakfast table. "Two good meals and you're back on track."

"Maybe it was just the change of scene. And looking at you."

"That, too. You going to check out Ms. Beadles Knox this morning?"

"First thing."

"Why don't I call and offer her a carpet-cleaning service to see if she's home."

"That would be good, Jack."

He opened his Manhattan phone book and dialed the number. After a generous wait, he hung up. "Sorry. The lady must work or walk the dog."

"I'll drop in on Arnold then. He probably has work I can do."

"I'll drive you to the station."

Jack's apartment is in Brooklyn Heights, which is just across the river from downtown Manhattan, where Arnold Gold's office is. The trip didn't take long, and I enjoyed the walk on the Manhattan side. Arnold's law office is in an old building with an elevator that has seen better days. When I walked into the reception area, I got a warm welcome. Yes, there was work, and no, Arnold hadn't gotten a temp for today. I took my coat off and got to work.

Arnold was off in court during the morning, but he returned after eleven, happy to see me. "So how about I take you to lunch, Chrissie?"

"Everybody's feeding me lately," I said. "Do I really look that bad?"

"You look terrific. I just don't feel like sharing my table with a member of the noble profession today. So if we get a table for two, my honorable colleagues will have to look elsewhere for scintillating conversation, of which, as you know, I am frequently a source. Also it's nice to be seen occasionally with a good-looking woman who isn't my wife."

"I accept."

Arnold's lunches are not anything that Hollywood or Wall Street would covet. But they're better than a sandwich and coffee at my desk, and the conversation is never disappointing.

"Well, you've been at it a couple of weeks now. Got a murderer yet?" he said when he had ordered.

"A lot of facts, a few conclusions, some suspects, but nothing I can pin on anyone. Opportunity but no real motive."

"I think you're damned good to learn anything after so long."

"In this case I had to find out who the victim was first. And although I haven't proved it conclusively yet with a dental X ray, I know who she was."

"OK. I'm waiting."

I told him about Candy, all the smiles caught by the Thurstons' camera, how she had come as a dreaded tenant and left as a member of the family. I told him how I could feel the exuberance of her spirit, her dedication as a teacher, her kindness as a friend, how the stories about her had made her live again for me.

I embellished my tale with the reminiscences of Mrs. Thurston and her daughter, Monica, and the warm recollections of Amy Broderick and her brother, Jerry Mulholland. " 'The delectable Miss Phillips,' he said," and I found my eyes misting.

"I see as usual you're taking this very personally."

"I started out wanting to give her a name so she could get a decent burial. But it's become more than that for me, Arnold. And it's not just that there were people, nice people, who loved her. Not just that there was some kind of hanky-panky going on in that town that everyone I've talked to would be happy to rebury. Not just that there are people who, for their own selfish reasons, have chosen to see her as unworthy."

Arnold's eyes pierced mine as they always do when he's

interested or concerned. "Then what is it?" he asked in a low voice.

"Candy was twenty-four years old when she died. Thirty years ago, when I was born, my mother was twenty-four. If they were alive today, they might have twenty-five or thirty-five years of life ahead of them. My mother's life was cut short by a disease for which there was no cure, and hard as that was for me, I came to accept it. But Candy's life was ended by someone who hated or feared her, and while there's no cure for that either, I want him exposed. Disease is fairly arbitrary. My mother had the bad luck to be stricken. But Candy was singled out for death. She died because of malice, and malice is hateful. I don't care if he's tried for his crime, but I want people to know he did it. I want people to know he isn't the wonderful person they think he is."

"Sounds like you know who did it."

"Well, of course I have my suspicions. But I can't for the life of me think why he would have done it. She was leaving the area. She already had a teaching job in another state. If they'd been having an affair, it was over."

"Maybe she was pregnant."

"She wasn't." I didn't explain, but he seemed to accept the forcefulness of my decree.

"Maybe he didn't do it."

I'm sure I heard myself sigh. "Then who did?" I asked, not rhetorically as it may have sounded but as a real question that cried for an answer.

"You've gone this far, you'll go all the way. Just eat hearty. You need to keep your strength up."

A few minutes after I got back to the office, Jack called. "She's there," he said. "I did my carpet-cleaning routine and got hung up on."

"You deserved it."

"I don't know why," he said with mock innocence. "I started out the way they all do: 'Hi, Mrs. Knox. How're you doing today?' "

"On my telephone, anyone who asks how I'm doing today is selling something."

"Well, maybe you've got a smoother approach than mine."

"I'll give it a try."

26

The subway took me uptown. I knew the area from recent visits to an old apartment house where a friend died. Joanne Beadles Knox lived in a prewar building between Broadway and Amsterdam Avenue. Like all the buildings of its vintage, it presented a monolithic facade flush with the sidewalk. I wonder sometimes why builders and planners totally excluded trees and greenery from their image of the city. One of the most refreshing things about going home is the smell of the air in Oakwood.

Once inside the outer lobby, I found her name on the panel and pressed her bell. There was no doorman, just a locked door between me and the inside lobby, and I needed someone to buzz me in.

"Yes?" a woman's voice called on the intercom.

"It's Christine Bennett," I called back. "Can I come up?" I said it because I couldn't think of anything else that would give me a greater chance of entry.

"Who?" she called back.

"Chris Bennett. Can I come in?"

There was a pause and then the buzzer sounded. I ran to the door and pushed it, feeling a surge of triumph. I had successfully negotiated the hardest part of my visit.

The Knoxes lived on the sixth floor, and the elevator took me up so smoothly, I was surprised. No one was looking out for me, so I found the apartment and pressed the bell.

"Who is it?" she said, opening a peephole in the door.

I was standing squarely in front of it so she could size me up. It's my firm conviction that I look unthreatening, "Christine Bennett."

She unbolted and opened the door a crack, and I saw the protective chain. "Do I know you?"

She was only a sliver of a woman, an eye and a nose, some hair colored a rather frightful red. "It's about your mother," I said.

I know that there are families torn apart by a hate so great that they engender murderous feelings, but I had met Joanne's mother, and I didn't think that hatred was the problem; I thought it was more likely misunderstanding. Whatever it was, I apparently said the right thing.

"My mother? Just a minute." She closed and reopened the door, this time wide enough for me to pass through. As I entered, I smelled a dinner cooking, and through the doorway to the kitchen, saw the implements of cooking on a counter.

Joanne Beadles Knox was a carbon copy of her mother except for the color of her hair. The daughter was a little taller, but she had the thin, almost bony build of her mother. I could have picked her out of a crowd without a picture. Even their voices were the same.

"Come on in," she said. "The kitchen's a little messy, but we can sit at the table." She was wearing a black wool skirt and a black sweater tucked inside it. Around her waist was a wide belt with a handsome buckle. Her stockinged feet were shod with heavy sneakers, as though she had kicked off her heels when she came home to cook and be comfortable.

The table in the dinette was round and clear except for a used coffee mug. She pushed it aside.

"You wanna give me your coat?"

"That's OK." I took it off and draped it on a chair.

"So what's this about my mother?"

"I saw her last week and she talked about you."

"You saw her?" She smiled as though she recognized the joke. "My mother is still alive?"

"She's been married to Mike Carpenter for a long time, and they live in a little house about twenty minutes from where she used to live."

"I don't know any Mike Carpenter."

"Mrs. Knox, I think your mother would like very much to see you again. I have her address here, and if you give me your permission, I'll give her yours."

"I don't know," she said. Her forehead had wrinkled. "Boy, would I like a cigarette right now, but I gave them up again two weeks ago and I've really been good."

That was all I needed, a little more guilt laid on me. "I really came to ask you about J.J. Eberling."

She put her hands on the edge of the table as though she were about to push herself away. Her nails were painted a deep red and looked well manicured. "Is he still alive?"

"No, he isn't, so you can talk freely."

"Who the hell are you, lady? You investigating me or something?"

"A body was found in the basement of the church in Studsburg," I said, feeling as though I'd said it so many times that the whole world ought to know about it by now. "Maybe you saw something on television."

"I did. A couple of weeks ago."

"I've been trying to find out who she is and who killed her. For a little while, I thought the body might be you."

She nodded and said, "Yeah. I'm glad it wasn't."

"One of the people I talked to was Darlene Jackson."

"Darlene," she said with a little smile. "I remember Darlene."

"She worked for the Eberlings before you did."

"Yeah. She told me about him. She warned me."

"I know that something happened. Can you tell me about it?"

"What does this have to do with the body?"

"I don't know. I'm trying to find out. Everyone I talk to from Studsburg just shuts up when I mention Mr. Eberling. Somehow I think you know something that no one else will tell me."

"I know something," she said.

I had thought she might volunteer, but instead she just sat and looked at me.

"Could you tell me about it? About Mr. Eberling?"

"He was rich and powerful and he got away with murder."

"Murder?"

"Well, I don't mean that for real. I mean he did what he wanted, and nobody stopped him."

"Like what?" I prompted.

"Like what he did to Darlene. He tried it with me, too, but I made him stop."

"How?"

"I just told him I wouldn't stand for it."

I was starting to feel the Studsburg runaround had extended to include her. I decided to be more direct. "Mr. Eberling gave you a lot of money."

"Who, me? He never gave me money."

"Your mother said—"

"My mother doesn't know. She never met him. She didn't know what was going on."

"What *was* going on?"

"I worked for them; he tried to . . . you know."

"Please, Mrs. Knox. A young woman was murdered. Something was going on in that town that no one will talk about. J.J. Eberling's dead now. He can't hurt you. J.J. Eberling gave you a lot of money. I need to know why."

"He didn't give me a cent that I didn't earn. That's it."

I felt weary and at the end of my patience. This was the person I had counted on to break the silence, to tell me something no one else would, to give me the scrap of information I needed to put everything I knew together and come up with an answer. Now she was stonewalling, too. "Mrs. Knox, you gave your mother ten hundred-dollar bills," I said, watching her face. "She put that money away for years because she thought you would come back and she wanted to give it to you, she wanted you to have it."

Her eyes were riveted on me, and as I watched, they formed tears. "She called me a whore," she said, her voice breaking and the tears spilling. "You know what it feels like when your own mother calls you that?"

I could only think how different were the recollections of the two parties to that terrible conversation. "She told me she loved you," I said. "She tried very hard to find you. If she said anything like that, she's paid for it a hundred times over. She saved the money for you. She didn't touch it till she and Mike bought the house. The money was her down payment. Please tell me why he gave it to you."

"The bitch," she said, reaching for a tissue. "She never told me in her whole life she loved me."

"She would tell you now."

"I don't want to hear it," she screamed. "When I needed it, it wasn't there. When I was a young kid and I wanted a mother, what did I have? You know what I said to her that last day? I said come with me. We'll go to New York together. We'll go anywhere together. I had enough to keep us going a long time."

"She's sorry now."

"Sure she's sorry. I thought she was dead till you came to the door. I tried to call her a long time ago—my husband said I should. She wasn't even listed. How did I know she got married?"

We sat quietly for a minute or two. I didn't know how to ask her again what I wanted to know. My question—my presence—had reopened the sorest wounds of her life, and it wasn't within my province to heal them. I felt terrible about what I'd done to her, and I'd lost my last good prospect for a lead to Candy's killer. I stood up and took my coat off the chair.

"You sure Eberling's dead?" she asked in a throaty voice.

"There's a death certificate in the county files."

"I heard something one night."

I sat down, my coat over my lap, my heart thumping.

"He had company for dinner, two men. It was a little after I started working there. She said she needed me till after dinner and could I stay. Someone would drive me home. It meant a couple of dollars more, so I stayed. The three of them went into his study after dinner. I brought them coffee and cigars. They were Cuban cigars, and you couldn't get them in those days because of Castro. But he had them. I could smell them when I went into the room.

"I was trying to keep out of their way," she went on. "I could see they were doing some kind of business. But Mrs. Eberling was nervous like. She wanted to make sure they had everything they needed, and she told me to go back and check if they wanted more coffee. When I went in, Mr. Eberling was handing an envelope to the general."

"A general? You mean in the army?"

"Yeah, in the army. He was in uniform and I saw the star on his shoulder."

"Could he have been Mr. Eberling's father?"

"No way. Mr. Eberling called him Bill a couple of times, and the other man called him General something, I don't remember what. Maybe Fitzpatrick or something like that."

"So Mr. Eberling was giving the general an envelope."

"And he dropped it when I came in, and it was money. I mean, it was more money than I'd ever seen in my whole life. Lots and lots of hundred-dollar bills."

"Like a payoff," I said.

"You bet it was a payoff. They were talking all night about that dam they were building and how it would work. And then there was the money."

"Mrs. Knox, do you remember the name of the third man in that room?"

"Oh yeah. His name was Fred Mayor. I wrote all these things down in case I needed them. I heard the general call him Mr. Mayor a couple of times. And Mr. Eberling called him Fred.''

The third man was Fred Larkin.

''You don't really have to tell me what happened after that,'' I said. It looked pretty plain to me, a simple case of extortion by a girl seizing on a situation that had fallen in her lap as the envelope of money had fallen on the table.

''It's not what you think,'' she said. ''I didn't start out to blackmail him. He really came to me and said I should live in a nice apartment, that I was too old to live with my mother. He got me a place that was furnished. I never even knew if he furnished it himself or he rented it that way. He said if I talked about what I'd seen that night, it could mean a serious embarrassment. That's how he put it. I was so dumb, I didn't even know what was going on in that town, that it was supposed to be flooded. But I could see there was something going on. Generals shouldn't be taking money like that. I was a little scared, but I knew enough to know that what I'd seen was worth something, more than just a furnished apartment. I knew the Eberlings were moving because they'd been talking about building a new house somewhere. I kept working there, but she told me it would be all over when they moved.''

''So you were out of a job then.''

''Right. So I talked to him one day—he used to be around during the day sometimes—and I told him I wanted to go to New York or someplace and I didn't have enough money. That's how I said it, that I needed some money to get started.''

''And he gave you the thousand dollars.''

She laughed. ''He gave me a hell of a lot more than that. He gave me five. I gave my mother one and kept the rest for myself. He also got me an apartment in New York. He didn't pay for it, he just told me where to go to find an apartment. I lived there till I got married and moved here.''

I told her I had gotten information from the super in her old building.

She shook her head. "How the hell did you find out about that place?"

I sketched it out for her.

She laughed again. "And I thought I covered my tracks pretty good."

"The super said someone beat you up while you were living there. I've been wondering about that."

She said, "Yeah," and lowered her eyes. "I got greedy. I figured if Eberling was good for five, he was good for ten. I wrote and asked for more money. I didn't hear from him till he showed up one night and beat the hell out of me. Cracked one of my ribs. He said if I ever asked for another cent or opened my mouth about what I'd seen, he'd kill me. I never did. I believed him."

She looked completely worn-out. I got up and put my coat on, thanked her for telling a story that she had hoped she would never have to repeat. Then I said, "About your mother."

"Get out," she said. "OK? I did my duty and told you what you want to know. It had nothing to do with any girl being killed. Now, would you please just get out?"

I took the elevator down and went outside. It had turned colder and meaner out. I turned toward Broadway where the subway was and started walking slowly, the pieces of information sliding into place, the gaps now fewer, my pulse rate probably higher. At Broadway I waited for the light. I was on the east side of the divided street, and downtown trains ran along the west side. As the light turned green, I stepped off the curb as someone behind me called, "Wait! Wait!"

At the divider, I turned to look behind me. Joanna Knox, dressed in a mink coat and the clunky sneakers, was running down the street, waving and calling, her red hair flying. I had just enough green left to make it back to the sidewalk.

Her eyes were streaming as she reached me, her makeup dissolving in rivulets. "I need the address," she said. "My mother. Do you still have her address? She has grandkids she never saw."

"Of course I do." I smiled, although I felt a little teary myself.

"I don't have a pencil or anything."

"I do." I took my steno book out of my bag, found a pen, and leafed through the pages till I found the address of Ginny Carpenter. I wrote it carefully, putting "Mike" in parens. "She really wants to see you."

"Thank you." She read the paper and nodded. "God bless," she said, and turned and walked back to her apartment.

27

"Are you thinking the same thing I am?" Jack said. He was changing his clothes for his law school class, and he had very little time.

"There was a payoff that had to do with the building of the dam."

"You said the mayor told you they'd fought the dam."

"Yes. But he said the little people never won those fights."

"What else could he say if he was in on the payoff?"

"When we took that walk on Sunday—"

"That's just what I'm thinking. There was a kind of natural basin upstream. If they had built the dam the other side of Studsburg, they wouldn't have had to flood a whole town and make five hundred people find new places to live. It sure as hell had to be a lot more expensive for the government than paying a couple of farmers for the value of their land. Could be Eberling and Larkin had big stakes in Studsburg, and this was their way of getting their money out."

"Maybe it was everybody's way out, Jack. Amy Broderick told me her father had been commuting to Rochester for a long time and they moved up there after they left Studsburg. I'll bet a lot of people wanted to sell and couldn't, and the dam represented a windfall. J.J. Eberling was an army brat. He could have known people very high up through his father, and he bribed this general to see to it that the dam was placed downstream of Studsburg instead of downstream of those farms and upstream of Studsburg."

"Sounds like it's falling into place." He reached into the closet and pulled out a tie. "How's this with my jacket?"

"Looks great to me. What do you need a tie for? You should see what the kids wear at the college I teach at."

"I am a law student, my dear. And what I lack in legal expertise, I make up for with my fashion wardrobe."

"You should never ask an ex-nun if something matches," I warned him. "Especially if she wore a habit. They're notorious for having no sense of what goes with what."

"You're different and I'm late. Give me one for the road."

We kissed and he picked up some notebooks and dashed for the door. "Hey, almost forgot to tell you. I got a call from Albany this afternoon. Your friend Degenkamp had a registered thirty-eight when he lived in Studsburg."

"Degenkamp?"

"Right."

"What about Larkin?"

"Nothing registered. And neither one has a registered handgun now. Lock up when you leave, and let me know where you are tomorrow."

"I will," I called as he bounded down the stairs. A little while later I drove home.

I called the Stiflers as soon as I got there and asked if I could come over. I had not told them that Henry Degenkamp had died, but they already knew. The younger Mrs. D. had called them, and they were planning to drive to Ithaca for the funeral on Friday.

"We'll be going tomorrow night," Carol said, "so we can stay over with Harry's mother and take her with us. From what we were told, his death sounds downright peculiar."

"It is," I agreed. "Henry got a call from Fred Larkin after I left the Larkins' house. Then Henry went out and they never saw him again."

"Something's really weird," Carol said.

"I have a favor to ask you, Harry. I'd like you to call your mother and ask her if the flooding of Studsburg was set up by Fred Larkin and J.J. Eberling so everyone in town could make some money."

"That's crazy," he said. "My folks loved that town."

"The house your mother lives in now. How does it compare with the one they left behind?"

"Well, it's better, but people always buy up a notch."

"Did they have much of a mortgage?"

He looked at me as though I'd just opened a door he'd never seen beyond. "I'll call my mother," he said.

"Tell her it was a long time ago and no one cares anymore. No one's going to be charged with anything. The principals are dead. I just want to know what went on."

It was a longer call than I had anticipated. While he was on the phone I went back over some of the little articles in the last issue of the *Herald*. Penny and Paul Armstrong settle in Arizona. Like all the other pieces, it was short and upbeat. Paul and Penny had bought themselves a great retirement home near Tucson. They had a dishwasher in the kitchen and the kind of stove Penny had always dreamed of. On the next page was a similar article about the Mulhollands. Their new house outside of Rochester had been completed in June and was ready for them to move into the day after they celebrated the christening and the Fourth. Further along was something about the mayor himself. He and Gwen were moving about sixty miles east to a wonderful house they had been remodeling over the last year. Everyone who ever lived in Studsburg was invited to visit. Included were their new address and telephone number. Three out of three sounded like they were doing a lot better after their move.

While I waited, I went back over the pictures. The Eberlings were there, the Larkins were there, the Degenkamps were there. There was no trace of Candy, night or day.

Harry finally got off the phone and came into the living room. "You know, I'm fifty-four years old and I've never heard my mother so rattled. Even when my father died, she held herself together, at least in public. But you're right, Kix. Something was going on that Carol and I never knew about."

"You weren't property owners," I said.

"That has to be it. And we were newly married, so we didn't care much what went on around us. It all started years before when there were studies about flooding and irrigation and water control. She said there was a natural place to dam up the water and put a couple of farms out of business, but J.J. Eberling came up with the idea that Studsburg should be flooded instead. But it was Fred Larkin who came around and talked to every family in town to see if they would go for it. Mom's pretty sure that J.J. benefited more than anyone else, but she said no one could have sold their house for what the government gave them. It sounds like it was a real sweet deal."

"Does she know how it was done?"

"All she knows is that J.J. handled it. Somehow he had a friendly ear in the army."

"That pretty much confirms what I learned today. And it means that Fred Larkin knew something that could send J.J. to jail. So when J.J. accidentally published something that Larkin found incriminating, he told J.J. to destroy the paper or else."

"But you've looked through the paper, Kix. There's nothing there but a bunch of boring articles on how Mr. and Mrs. Somebody are doing in their new home. And how does it tie in to the schoolteacher?"

"I think she found out about the payoff to flood Studsburg and she threatened to expose Larkin and J.J."

"It doesn't square with what Mom told me. We talked about that, too. She admitted she knew something was going on between the mayor and the new schoolteacher, but she didn't think it had anything to do with the dam being built. From what she said, I gather my father talked to Fred about the rumors, and Fred said it was a personal matter and not to worry about the dam. He also told Dad to mind his business.''

I went home a little while later. With all that I knew, there had to be one major piece missing from the puzzle. Henry Degenkamp's death, even if the result of natural causes, was suspicious. Gwen Larkin's death in a single vehicle accident was equally suspicious. And both people had a close relationship to Fred Larkin.

And now I knew that Henry had owned a .38-caliber revolver. Had he committed the murder or had he given the gun to Larkin? Larkin had said something to Henry on the telephone on Monday, and in some way that had caused Henry's death. A threat? A warning? I didn't think I had a chance in the world of finding out anything from Larkin. In fact, my sources of information were drying up. Henry was dead, Eberling was dead, Larkin wouldn't tell me anything and might be dangerous to boot.

Before I went to bed, I called Jack and told him what old Mrs. Stifler had finally admitted to. I said I would probably go upstate in the morning. Maybe I'd do this, maybe I'd do that. In any case, I wanted to convey my condolences to Ellie Degenkamp. Jack remarked that I didn't sound hopeful and assured me something would break; it always did. I hoped he was right.

28

Ithaca had a layer of new snow, and Cayuga Heights looked like something out of a picture book. The streets were freshly plowed and most of the sidewalks had been shoveled, at least one snow shovel's width, but lawns were clean white blankets, and trees stretched out branches with an even two inches of white. But the fairy tale ended at the Degenkamps' doorstep. Several cars were parked at the curb and across the street, and as I turned off my motor, an old woman in a dark coat and clumsy boots was just leaving their house. The younger Mrs. Degenkamp was seeing her out.

I'm not any better at these occasions than anyone else is. I just gear myself up, knowing that the people I visit will take some comfort from my presence. As I got out of the car, an elderly couple came out of the house. I waited till they had made their cautious way down the long slate walk to their car and then went to the door. It was opened by the younger Mrs. D.

"Miss Bennett," she said with surprise. "Please come in. Have you had a long drive?"

I told her I had and asked if the funeral would be the next day, as scheduled.

"Yes, they've done an autopsy, although my mother-in-law wasn't very happy about it. It was what they suspected, a heart attack coupled with exposure. We have no idea what made him park his car and go walking on such a cold day."

She took me to the living room, where a handful of mostly older people were sitting with Ellie. Eric Degenkamp, his

wife said, was at the funeral home, making some final ar-
rangements. He would be back soon.

Ellie recognized me and shook my hand. "It was a heart
attack," she said. "He must have felt it coming on and got
out of the car to get help. He was sitting next to a tree when
they found him."

"I'm so sorry," I said.

"He shouldn't've gone out. It was too cold. But you can't
tell a grown man anything."

"I think he liked his independence," I said.

"He did. He was a very independent man, my Henry."

Eric walked in just then and went to whisper something to
his mother. I moved away and found a seat next to a woman
who looked very old and very healthy. We introduced ourselves and she said, "I'm ninety-three years old."

"You look wonderful," I said honestly.

"That's what comes of living in Ithaca for sixty years.
People live long, healthy lives in Ithaca."

We made small talk for a few minutes and she insisted I
sample the cookies she had baked that morning. When she
left a few minutes later, I decided I had stayed long enough
myself. I went to Ellie to say good-bye.

"You think Fred said something to him?" she asked me.
"You think he brought on Henry's heart attack?"

"I don't know, Ellie. I hope not. Fred didn't tell you anything when you called that day?"

"He didn't say anything at all to me. He wasn't home. It
was his wife I talked to. She said Fred had gone out. He left
after he called Henry."

I tried to keep my face from showing my surprise. If Fred
had left his house after he called Henry, he could have been
ten minutes behind me on the way to Ithaca, and the two men
could have met while I was at the Degenkamp home. It looked
as though I had begun to penetrate Fred Larkin's fortress and
he had driven to Ithaca to warn Henry to keep quiet about
something.

"You think Henry went out to meet him?" Ellie asked.

"I think it's possible."

"I thought this was all over a long time ago," she said.

"I need someone to talk to me about it," I said softly.

"Not me," she said. "I'm finished talking. You know who to see."

"I don't."

"Who do people tell their secrets to?"

I stared at her.

"Ask him about the time capsule," she said. "See what he says." She pressed her lips together, then relaxed. "Thank you for coming, Christine."

Her daughter-in-law walked me to the door. "She's holding up very well. My father-in-law's health wasn't very good, and he never took care of himself the way the doctor said he should."

She opened the door for me and I stepped outside. At the foot of the walk an old blue car was parked. Something about it struck me. I stood looking at it, trying to remember.

"Is something wrong?" Mrs. D. called from the doorway.

"Whose car is that?"

"It was my father-in-law's. Eric just used it to go to the funeral home."

"Did your in-laws drive that car to Studsburg a couple of weeks ago for the baptism?"

"I'm sure they did. He loved that car. He'd never drive anything else."

"Thank you," I said.

It was the car I'd seen parked at the edge of Studsburg when I made my late afternoon visit to St. Mary Immaculate and stumbled on Candy Phillips's body. Either Henry Degenkamp had opened the grave or he knew who did because he saw him.

I got in my car and drove to the nearest pay phone.

29

Carol Stifler answered her phone on the second ring. I asked her to get the *Herald*, and when she came back I told her I wanted to hear the article about Father Hartman. Pages turned as I wondered how long the old newsprint would survive the abuse we were giving it.

"Got it," she said. " 'Father Hartman Looks To the Future.' "

"That's it. I'm listening."

" 'Father Gregory Hartman is looking forward to a year at least at the chancery in Rochester. While a city of three hundred thousand will mean quite a change from a parish of two hundred forty-seven, Father Hartman is sure—' Is this really what you want to hear, Kix?"

"Skip to the next paragraph."

" 'Father's apartment in the rectory of Saint—' "

"Try the next one."

" 'On another note, Father Hartman's interest in the future extends beyond his work in Rochester and beyond the millennium. Before he leaves Studsburg for the last time on July fifth, he will bury a mint set of coins in the basement of St. Mary Immaculate.' Oh my God," Carol said. "I don't think I ever read this."

"Go on, Carol."

" 'While it is unlikely that anyone will ever uncover the coins, Father believes that God has mysterious ways. "There are floods like the great flood in the Old Testament and there are droughts," he told this reporter. "The waters parted once, they may part again in another era. Who knows whether Studsburg will remain underwater forever? For that future archeologist, whenever he happens upon them, these coins will remind him of the year this town ceased to exist, of the civilization it was part of, of the people who loved living here.''

" 'This reporter can only hope that favored person steps softly among the memories.' That's it, Kix. I don't believe what I've just read. You aren't telling me Father Hartman—''

"No, I don't think he killed anyone. Thanks, Carol. I have some traveling to do.''

"Oh, Christine, I'm feeling very scared.''

I wasn't feeling very calm myself.

It is well know that the confessional is sealed. If someone had confessed to Father Hartman that he had killed Candy Phillips, I would expect that the priest would listen, instruct him in the strongest terms to turn himself in, and give him conditional absolution, the condition being that the penitent do what the priest told him to do. The priest might offer assistance and prayer, but he would never discuss the content of the confession with another person.

So it was not with great optimism that I pulled into the driveway of Father Hartman's rectory. But now that I knew some of the relevant questions to ask, there was a chance that he had knowledge acquired outside the confessional, and he might be willing to share it with me.

There was a parishioner in his office when I arrived, and I took a seat in the outside room. The housekeeper asked me if I wanted a cup of coffee, but I turned her down. As I sat waiting, a young curate in a cassock came down the stairs, said a cheery hello, and left by a side door. It was probably his turn to hear confessions in the church across the driveway from the rectory.

While I waited, I tried to assemble the facts I had collected piecemeal from the *Herald* and the many people I had interviewed. It seems amazing sometimes how tiny snippets of information from diverse informants with a variety of axes to grind can add up to a solution, even a complex one, like a lot of small streams coming together to form a mighty river.

The door opened and Father Hartman and a young, troubled-looking man came out.

"Christine," the priest said with a warm smile. "How nice to see you." He walked the young man to the door, patted him on the shoulder, and came back to me.

"Do you have time for a few questions?"

"You bet. Come on in."

It was small and homey with a fireplace and old furniture. Father Hartman took a seat on a chair instead of behind his desk, and I sat more or less opposite him.

"I'm afraid no luck on your initials," he said.

For a moment I forgot what he was talking about. Then I remembered the medal. "This is about something else. About the time capsule."

He smiled. "The time capsule, yes. The time capsule that wasn't. Where did you hear about it?"

"It was written up in the last issue of the *Studsburg Herald*."

He looked puzzled. "There was no last issue. I mean, J.J. Eberling promised one for the fifth of July, but he came by and said there wasn't any, he was sorry, it just hadn't worked out."

"He put it together, printed it at the Steuben Press, and started to give them out at the bridge on Main Street. Someone stopped him."

"I see."

"Can you tell me about the capsule, Father?"

"It was just a little idea I had. I'd always been fascinated by those capsules they buried at famous places like the World's Fair and the Times Building. I thought there might come a time when Studsburg emerged from the depths, possibly even a time when St. Mary Immaculate crumbled and fell. I thought there should be something there to remind a future generation that this lake was once a town, that it died in a certain year, that Americans lived there. I wrote to the treasury or the mint, I forget exactly, and ordered a mint set of coins. My intention was to bury them in the basement of the church on that last morning.''

"Did you?''

"I couldn't. I had opened up a hole in a wall under the stairs a day or so earlier, and I had mortar and whatever else the hardware store sold me so I could seal it up again. I hadn't said anything about it till J.J. Eberling came to me for my exit interview, so to speak.''

"And you told him about it then.''

"That's right. And about my plans for the next year. The last issue was supposed to be a kind of compendium of everybody's future plans and pictures from the picnic and fireworks. But he said he ran into some obstacle and couldn't get it published.''

"What about your time capsule?''

"I went to the church that last morning and celebrated my last mass, feeling very sad and very nostalgic, as I'm sure you can appreciate. Then I went back to the rectory and finished my packing. We had to leave the town by noon, and a few people dropped by to say a last good-bye, although we'd done that the night before. It must have been around that time that J.J. Eberling dropped in and said he was sorry, there wouldn't be any final edition of the *Herald*.''

"Did he seem upset?'' I asked.

"J.J. was one of those men who existed behind a smooth veneer. I heard those rumors you mentioned, that there had been incidents involving him with a teenage girl. Nothing ever fazed him. I expect he died without a line of worry on his face. There was something almost unreal about him. Maybe that's why I never tried to develop a personal relationship with him. It certainly wasn't because he wasn't a member of my parish. I was on very friendly terms with a Jewish family in town. They used to invite me to their Friday evening dinner sometimes and substitute fish for their usual chicken. That was before John the Twenty-third, of course."

"And the capsule," I prompted.

"It must have been eleven o'clock by the time I took the coins and went back to the church. I had them in a metal box I'd picked up somewhere. I couldn't bury anything besides metal because of the water. I went in the back way, as I usually did—the door was near the rectory—and went down to the basement to put the box in the opening and seal it up, but somebody had done it for me. The sealing material was gone and the wall was solid. I was at a loss. I looked around, expecting someone to pop out of the shadows and yell 'Surprise!' But no one was there. I decided someone must have played a joke on me and I left it at that. I had no idea what the purpose of the prank was."

"Until someone confessed to you that he had killed the schoolteacher."

"You know I can't respond to that."

"Yes, I do know." I was certain now that I was right. If he had not known, he would have denied it. There would have been no reason for him not to. "What happened to the coins?" I asked.

"I took them with me. I'd broken the sealed package they were displayed in to put them in the box. When I got to Rochester, I was able to find a picture framer to set them up again." He nodded toward the wall behind me. "They're right over there"

I went and looked. The familiar coins were still bright and shiny, pure and untouched. His idea of burying them had been a good one. Made of metal, they would not have bounced around much, not sustained damage.

"Have you heard that Henry Degenkamp is dead?" I asked, returning to my chair.

"I got a phone call. They said it was a heart attack."

"Father, Henry died because he knew who murdered Candy Phillips."

He shook his head slowly. "You know better than this, Chris."

"I'm not asking you to tell me what you aren't allowed to tell me. I'm asking for guidance. Even if I can't bring this man to justice, I want him exposed."

"I'll tell you whatever I know that I've learned outside the confessional."

"Fred Larkin and Candy Phillips were lovers. Gwen Larkin found out about it, and Fred killed Candy the night of the fireworks. He probably lured her there with some kind of promise. She had already left Studsburg at the end of the semester and she came back for the Fourth of July. After he killed her, his relationship with his wife deteriorated. Less than a year later he rigged her car and she went off the road and hit a tree and died. After it happened, he never told anyone from Studsburg except his closest friends that she was dead."

"I knew she was dead," the priest said. "And if Fred killed her, he didn't tell me, and I don't believe he did. I think he loved Gwen. While they were married, I don't think there was another woman in his life. I don't for one moment believe that he and the schoolteacher were lovers. I'm sorry to say that just about everything you believe to be true is false, Chris. If that's the guidance you need, I hope it helps you."

"Father, she was beautiful and happy and twenty-four years old. Everyone in that town that I've talked to has been uncooperative because they were all involved in a scam. Every homeowner in Studsburg benefited from it, whether they knew there'd been a payoff or not. If Candy and Larkin weren't lovers, then maybe she was blackmailing him or threatening to expose him for his part in the scam."

Father Hartman looked down at the table in front of him, then raised his eyes to meet mine. "You're right. There was a scam, and the whole town was part of it. It's possible she knew. At some point it was talked about almost openly. There were people who were euphoric at the prospect of the buy-out. I heard about it, as you can imagine. Not owning property, I was a completely disinterested party, and I chose to stay out of the whole affair. During the years I served in Studsburg, many people tried to sell their homes, especially older people who had retired and wanted to move somewhere warmer. Studsburg had been a dying town for many years. Their industry had dried up and there were no expectations for anything new coming in. When the possibility of a government buy-out appeared, there was almost a mass hysteria. People saw a way out from the bondage of real estate. Oh, there were a few diehards, but they were won over very quickly. The prospect of quick, easy money was just too attractive for anyone to turn down. The number of people with uneasy consciences was very small." He said it with sadness, as if his ministry had failed to overcome greed, one of the seven deadly sins.

"I guess I'm not surprised," I said. "They were ordinary people, and it didn't take much to convince themselves they deserved a windfall."

"That's certainly how they looked at it."

He hadn't really responded to my suggestion that Candy was angry enough at the scam that she might be threatening to expose Larkin if he didn't get the town out of it. I took the sixth grade picture out of my bag, opened the folder, and laid it on the table in front of Father Hartman.

He looked at it almost sadly, then smiled. "That's the little Mulholland girl in the front row."

"Amy Broderick. She gave me the picture last week."

"Her brother was quite a handful."

"He said that at thirteen he was madly in love with Miss Phillips."

"With all their faults, they were a wonderful parish." He handed the picture back to me and rose. "I think I've given you all the guidance I can, Chris. What will you do now?"

I had been wondering the same thing. "I have only two options left. I think I'll sleep on it."

* * *

I arrived at Sacred Heart too late for dinner, but one of the nuns helped scrape together a sandwich for me, and there was ice cream in the freezer. I sat at a counter in the kitchen and ate while I tried to sort out what I had learned today. I found that I was convinced that no one in Studsburg—except the murderer and perhaps one other person—knew that Candy had been killed. Even the handful of people like the younger Stiflers who had received the last issue of the *Herald* had no reason to think the young schoolteacher had met with foul play. She had simply left the town, and they had never seen her again. *But they all knew that something was going on between Candy and Larkin.* And they were all covering for him, and it had to be because they owed him. But Father Hartman seemed very certain that Candy and Larkin had not been lovers. Which left only a threat and a deadly retaliation.

Or did it? After washing my dishes, I went up to my mirrorless room and sat in the chair with my notes on my lap. Suddenly the contrast between a nun's cell and a secular woman's bedroom seemed starker than I had ever observed. For all that I am a quiet, somewhat introverted person, at home I frequently reach outward. I call Jack because I want to hear his voice. I adjust my morning walk so that I will run into Melanie Gross and have the opportunity to talk to her. I call her sometimes at night to let her know I am still her friend and neighbor even though I haven't seen her for a while. I turn on the radio or television set to bring the outside world into mine.

But the nuns turn inward. There is a lamp on the desk that can be turned on or off, a window shade that can be pulled up or down. The outside world that the window lets in is the same slice every day, varied only by seasons and weather. There is no phone at your fingertips, and after a fairly early hour, there is also no conversation. There is only introspection.

Eventually that night, it began to work for me. After I had gone over my notes several times, I turned off the overhead light and flicked off the lamp. I pulled the window shade up as far as it would go and looked out over the dark landscape. Here, too, there had been some snow, although not much. But there was a moon out tonight, and my eyes quickly adjusted to the meager light, taking in the white overlay, the shadowy trees, the distant chapel, the miniature hills and valleys of the convent's property. And as I looked at the clean, snowy fields, thinking and not thinking, I heard the echo.

People say things, but the message doesn't always penetrate. Like raindrops on a well-waterproofed raincoat, the words just sit there, round and clear and transparent. Eventually, if they stay long enough, if no one brushes them away, they're soaked up; the message hits its mark.

What was it Father Hartman had said about Fred and Gwen Larkin? I listened to the echo several times and then pulled down the shade.

I had told Father Hartman I had two options left. I could go back and rehash everything with Fred Larkin, who might well throw me out this time. Or I could explore the only lead I had that was completely new.

The choice was pretty clear.

30

Scranton is a sizable town in northeastern Pennsylvania, but the forwarding address I had from the post office for Candy Phillips was suburban, much like the little New York State town she had lived in the year she taught in Studsburg. I stopped at the police station and asked for directions. The street, at least, still existed.

So did the house. It was a very different style from the last one she had lived in, older and larger, rambling and veran-daed, the kind that can easily be made into a boarding house or rescued by an energetic couple anxious to gentrify the neighborhood. As I approached the door, I heard a piano, played by someone with considerably more talent than a child doing études. Out of respect, I waited till the music stopped to ring the bell.

The door was opened by a thin, stooped old man who looked me up and down and then said, "The room's gone."

"I'm not looking for a room. I'm looking for someone who lived here."

"Who's that?"

"Candy Phillips."

"Don't remember any Candy, don't remember any Phillips."

"It was a long time ago. She may not have been here long."

A woman appeared, holding a dust mop. "I can take care of it, Dad. Go back to your music." She gave me a smile from a plump, bespectacled face. "I'm afraid we let the room last night. If you'd like to leave your name—"

I told her my name and repeated my mission. She shook her head, said she was Helen Little, and said Candy's name didn't ring a bell. I asked her how long her family had lived there.

"A long time. My parents bought the house after the war."

"This young woman was going to teach somewhere lo-cally. She probably took a room for a year or at least for the academic year. It was about thirty years ago, maybe a few months more than that."

Her eyes narrowed. "Did she stay the year?"

"She probably only stayed a few days or a week." The piano playing had begun again, something melodic that I thought might be Chopin.

I must have smiled, because she said, "My father loves to play."

I took the sixth grade picture out of my bag and showed it to her.

"It's hard to remember a face after so long," she said. "But I do remember that someone took a room when I was a kid and then went away."

"Did she leave any luggage?"

Her face brightened and she gave me a big grin. "Come with me," she said.

I followed her to the kitchen and then down a flight of stairs to the basement. It looked like most basements that have endured a single owner for many decades. Old, useless furniture that no one wanted and no one could part with was stashed in one section. Garden equipment was stored in another. Cartons of who knew what were piled wherever they fit.

"I'd completely forgotten those suitcases," she said, "but I know they're here. We got a flood one year, and I remember putting them on top of something."

"Did you ever look inside?"

"I just don't remember. Maybe my father did."

We both started looking, but she came up with them first. "Success!" she called. "Here's one." She lifted it and set it down on top of a carton. "And here's the other. Not bad." She looked triumphant.

"Not bad at all. Would you mind if I opened them?"

"Open them, take them away, do anything you want. If there's any money in them—"

"I doubt there is, but why don't you watch while I go through the contents."

We each carried one upstairs and set them down in the large, homey kitchen. The lock on the larger one was locked, and we broke it open with a screwdriver. Inside were most of Candy Phillips's clothes and little else. I stuck my hands in the pockets along the sides but found nothing except a pair of nylon stockings, probably worn and not yet washed, a wad of fresh tissues, and a pair of black leather gloves lined with wool.

The smaller suitcase was the train case with the mirrored top that Monica Thurston had described. It wasn't locked, and that was where the great secrets of Candida Phillips's life were neatly stored. As I removed a thick manila envelope, Mrs. Little's father came into the kitchen.

"Was that that girl where the letters went back and forth?"

"That would be the one," I said.

"They sent 'em here, she never came back, I sent 'em there, they came back again."

"Do you know what happened to them?"

"They're in there somewhere. I put 'em in before I threw the bags in the basement. You'll find 'em."

I wished desperately I were alone. I wanted to uncover the details of Candy's life in privacy, as though I were unclothing her. It seemed indecent for two strangers to stand by and watch something so intimate. As for me, in the course of the last two and a half weeks, I had become her spiritual surrogate.

"Go ahead, you'll find 'em," the old man urged.

"Leave her alone, Dad," his daughter said gently. Then to me, "What happened to her?"

"She died the day after she left here."

"How terrible. And no one knew?"

"Her body was hidden."

I pulled everything out of the envelope and put it on the table. I could feel Helen Little over my shoulder.

She laughed. "Well, if there isn't any money, I'm not interested."

"You think there's money?" her father asked.

"Doesn't look like it, Dad. I thought maybe we'd come into a windfall." She moved away from the table, and her father left the kitchen. A minute later, I heard the piano.

There were two teaching licenses, one for Pennsylvania and one for New York. There were pictures of her from infancy through to the end of her life. The sixth, seventh, and eighth grade photos from Studsburg were there. Her mother was in several older pictures, a pretty woman who looked very much like her daughter. I found Candy's diploma from Penn State along with several letters from Studsburg, copies of which I had seen in the county files, and from the school she had intended to teach in the fall after she was murdered.

There was also a letter that I assumed to have been written to her mother. It was from the office of the registrar of Syracuse University, and it said she could reapply for admission at any time with no prejudice. It was dated twenty-five years before the end of Studsburg. If Candy's mother had ever reapplied, there was no indication of it among the papers. There was a Pennsylvania driving license for Shirley Phillips, a social security card, a library card, a birth certificate, a charge account card for a department store I had never heard of, but no college diploma.

In a smaller envelope there were receipts of paid hospital bills, nursing bills, doctor bills, and pharmacy bills, all from the last year of Shirley Phillips's life, the year before her daughter came to Studsburg. I flipped through the record of a woman's last months of life, feeling her despair and the heartache of her daughter.

There wasn't much else, but I had found what I came for. As I put the papers back in the large envelope, the music stopped again and the old man came back into the kitchen.

"You find those letters?"

"Not yet."

"She's the one that left the typewriter," he said. "When she didn't come back for it, I gave it to my daughter. You want that, too?"

"No, thanks. I don't need it."

He left the room, and I reached into the elasticized pocket along the back of the train case. In it were several letters rubber-banded together. A few were from the school she was going to teach in, probably from an increasingly anxious principal wondering where his fall teacher was. They had been sent to this address, readdressed to her last New York address, and returned again by the post office. The other two letters had both been sent to Candida Phillips at her address near Studsburg. Both had been readdressed to come here, then addressed again to go back to her last address. Finally they were addressed one last time by the post office to come here again. Musical chairs.

I looked at the return addresses, feeling a combination of sadness and success. The middle initial was M.

Mrs. Little poked her head into one of the doorways to the kitchen. "Find anything?"

"Nothing of value but the papers. Do you mind if I take them?"

"Take everything, why don't you?"

"I will. Mrs. Little, if I give you five dollars, would you let me call New York?"

"Go ahead," she said breezily. "Don't worry about the money. You should see what I spend calling my daughter."

I dialed Jack's number at the precinct. He wasn't at his desk, but someone went looking and he picked up the phone.

"Sergeant Brooks."

"Jack, it's Chris."

"Hi. What's up?"

"I've got it all now. There's just one document I'd like to research. Do you think you can get me a birth certificate from fifty-seven years ago?"

"What city?"

"Erie, Pennsylvania," I said, reading from the address on the letter from Syracuse. "Candida Phillips. The mother's name was Shirley."

"Anything special you want to know?"

"The father's name."

"I'll call you tonight. You be at the convent?"

"Yes."

"Talk to you then."

I left a five on the table and took the suitcases to the car.

I was sitting with the nuns in the community room when he called. The television set was on, but only one or two were watching. Some were reading the paper, one doing embroidery, one writing a letter. I had told them I was pretty sure I knew who and why, and I was sorry, I couldn't talk about it. When I was called to the phone, I was glad to leave them.

"OK," Jack said without introduction. "You were right on the year and the mother. I can't help you on the father. It's recorded as unknown. I take it that doesn't surprise you."

"It doesn't surprise me at all."

"So where to now?"

"To see the father," I said.

31

Fred Larkin opened the front door and stood barring my way in. "I think we've had our last conversation, Miss Bennett. So if you'll just turn yourself around and get in your car and go back to where you came from, we'll both be better off."

"You were Candy's father," I said.

His face changed. An eyelid throbbed. He said nothing, but he didn't move. Finally he said, "That's a lot of nonsense and you know it. You say anything about this and I'll sue you for everything—"

"I've seen her birth certificate." Another lie, but in a good cause.

"Keep your voice down," he said angrily.

"Then talk to me. A New York City policeman has all the documentation ready to turn over to the sheriff's office."

He looked around as though his nonexistent neighbors

might be gathering nearby to hear my defamation of him. "Come inside, and don't say a word till I tell you."

I followed him into the room with the aerial photo and the trophies. He left me there and went to talk to his wife. While he was gone, I found the framed diploma he had gotten from Syracuse University in the year of Candy's birth. I was standing in front of it when he came in and closed the door behind him. A moment later I heard the outside door close as his wife left the house, sent, no doubt, on a useless errand.

"I'm sure you didn't know she was your daughter when you interviewed her for the teaching job," I said.

"I didn't."

"Phillips is a fairly common name, and she didn't live in Erie, where Shirley had lived." I watched him flinch as I said the name. "So I assume she told you while she was teaching."

"She did."

"And she wanted something from you because you had never acknowledged her." And probably never helped her mother, I thought without saying it.

"She wanted something I couldn't give her," Larkin said miserably.

"Something you couldn't give her. So you lured her to the church on the Fourth of July and killed her during the fireworks. You knew Father Hartman had opened a vault in the wall downstairs, and to make it easier, he had even left the sealing material down there. All you had to do was shoot her and stuff her body in the opening, knowing it would never be found. When you saw the article in the *Herald* the next day, with the piece about Father Hartman's time capsule, you made J.J. Eberling stop distributing the paper."

"Where did you find that paper?" His face furrowed into deep lines that hadn't been there before, as though all the worries of a lifetime had descended upon him at this moment to take their toll.

"J.J. distributed a few copies before you stopped him."

"That bastard. After all the favors I'd done for him over

the years, all the rough edges I'd smoothed over, he fought with me about that paper."

"That paper was very important to him," I said. "He'd promised it to everyone in town. They were all looking forward to driving down Main Street for the last time and picking up the yearbook edition of the *Herald*."

"You're right about that. He saw it as his swan song."

"By the way, the Degenkamps saw you fighting with J.J. that morning. They knew it was about the paper, because he wouldn't give them a copy when they asked, and he had a stack of them right there. And Henry Degenkamp knew who opened the grave in the basement of St. Mary Immaculate. You drove to Ithaca last Monday after I talked to you to warn him to keep quiet. He died a few hours later."

"And I suppose I'm responsible for that, too. You listen to me, young lady. You may have found out I was Candy's father, but you haven't got another thing right, and you'll never prove I killed her, because I didn't."

It came to me in a replay of a moment a few evenings earlier. In the pictures in the *Herald* I had only tried to pinpoint Larkin. Now I could see as though it were in front of me a nighttime photo with Gwen Larkin's place at the table empty.

"Your wife killed her," I said.

He slumped into a leather chair. "I fathered a child and I never acknowledged her," he said. "I gave Shirley a hundred dollars, which was a lot of money in the thirties, believe me. I didn't have any more. She left school and I never saw her again. Twenty-four years later, a teacher showed up and claimed to be my daughter. There was nothing I could do. If I tried to get rid of her, she would make our relationship public. I was on tenterhooks that whole year. Finally she had the gall to go to my wife and tell her I was her father."

"The gall to say who her father was," I said softly.

"She had no right to destroy my wife's life," he raged.

"So your wife killed her. Did she use Degenkamp's gun?"

"It wasn't like that." He ran his hand through his thick

silver hair. "Candy was the one who did the luring. I was supposed to meet her in the church basement during the fireworks. I suppose she came back from wherever she'd gone to. But Gwen said she'd go instead, that if she told Candy she couldn't be embarrassed by the disclosure, maybe she'd just go away and leave us in peace. It was Candy who brought the gun. They fought over it, and Gwen got it and shot her. Then she shoved the body in the opening and sealed it up. She took Candy's purse so nothing was in there to identify her in case the engineers accidentally opened the grave. She kept the damn thing in the house. I used to come home and see her going through it. The shooting made her crazy. That's the truth of it. She started drinking. One night in the winter, she took the car and ran it into a tree. After the funeral I burned the purse." He closed his eyes.

"And the gun?" I asked.

"I disposed of it. I went to a city dump and threw the parts in. It's gone."

No one would ever know what it was that made Gwen Larkin crazy. Perhaps it was the shooting. Perhaps it was all the revelations of that year, that her husband had had a lover, that he had fathered a child, that he had abandoned both the mother and the daughter, that someone might find out. I found myself believing his story that Gwen had committed the murder, but neither the way it happened nor whose gun it was, but the questions were moot. I had reached a point where I so identified with Candy that I could not imagine her to be murderous. And even if she had had a gun, I couldn't believe she would ever have used it.

"What did she want from you?" I asked.

"It doesn't matter anymore. It's over. It's gone."

"I suppose it was about the payoff to the general," I said, watching his eyebrows rise, his eyes widen. "Everyone in town knew something was going on between you and Candy, but no one would say anything because of the deal you and J.J. Eberling made to get the town flooded."

"You know about that."

"Even today, Mr. Larkin, they pretend they don't know who Candy was, that you weren't seen with her in your car."

"Then how do you know?"

"I talked to the children. The children loved her."

"I could have loved her," he said, "if she hadn't been so angry. I did everything I could to make it right. Nothing worked. You think I'm a bad person. It wasn't like that. I was a young man, a boy, away at school. The girl I loved was somewhere else. I longed for her and I transferred my affections momentarily to someone else. I had no intention to ruin her life. I gave her the money to help her—to do something. What happened afterward was a nightmare. It ruined her life, her daughter's, my wife's, even mine. Everyone lost."

"Except the people of Studsburg. They were all winners, weren't they?"

"Leave it alone, Miss Bennett. It's all over now."

"Not quite," I said. Then I left.

32

I paid the nuns what I thought fair and what they thought was bountiful. Then I bought a hefty supply of their jams and drove home. I called Deputy Drago and told him to try to find a dentist for Candida Phillips at the last address she had lived in in Pennsylvania before coming to Studsburg. Within a few days he had a match. I didn't tell him anything else.

After the body was identified, Fred Larkin claimed it as mayor of Studsburg and gave Candy the burial she deserved.

I attended, although he was less than happy about it, and when I tried to pay for part of the cost, he said he had taken care of it himself. He and I and a local priest were the only people in attendance.

On one day when I had the time, I called Ginny Beadles Carpenter and found out she had already heard from Joanne. She thanked me with some emotion. I called Mrs. Thurston and told her that the X rays confirmed what we suspected about Candy. We had a nice talk and I sent my regards to Monica.

I called Amy Mulholland Broderick and told her much the same thing. The day before, I had slipped the sixth grade photo into a strong cardboard envelope and mailed it back to her.

The toughest call to make was to her brother.

"Why would anyone ever want to kill a doll like that?" he said.

"It was very complicated," I told him. "It involved old indiscretions and new greed."

"Greed, I can understand," he said lightly.

"Greed, it was," I said.

I visited my cousin Gene at the Greenwillow residence for retarded adults, bringing him several miniature cars for his collection to make up for my absence of several weeks. Gene is very forgiving, and I suspect I always get more out of my visits than he does.

Melanie and I made a date for dinner, and Jack drove up and met the Grosses in a happy Saturday night get-together that we all enjoyed. And one afternoon I got a call from Carol Stifler that Maddie and the baby were there and could I come right over. Between bouncing and crooning, I asked Carol to send a message to old Mrs. Stifler that if the rains ever came, I wanted to know about it before the church was completely submerged. She promised to let me know.

The snows came before the rains, inches and then feet of it upstate. It was evening-out time for the weather. With the first thaw, a heavy rain came. One evening Carol Stifler called and said the word upstate was that only the steeple was still visible, and with the river rising, it wasn't likely to be seen much longer.

I got a huge supply of Jack's sister's chicken and mushrooms and a chocolate cake as well and brought it up to the convent one afternoon, having told them it and I were coming. We feasted happily, finishing off with the wonderful cake. The next morning, after prayers and breakfast, I drove to Studsburg for the last time.

The little sign with the arrow had washed out, but I recognized the road to the old town. The rain had stopped, but there was a tremendous runoff according to the local weather forecaster, and the church would be completely underwater very soon, even without additional precipitation.

Although it was a weekday, there were a handful of cars parked near the basin rim. There was even a van with the call letters of a local TV station. I got out and walked the last hundred or so feet. Below me was a lake, still well short of its bank, but deep enough to have hidden any trace of the town except for the cross of the steeple of St. Mary Immaculate. I felt a terrible sadness, for Candy, for her killer, for all the people driven by greed who had helped in their tiny ways to make her death happen. Way off beyond the Simpsons' farm I could see the river water backing up into the lake. The payoff dam was doing its duty.

"I thought you might come."

I turned without surprise to see Father Hartman. "I hoped you would be here."

"I was here the first time the church went underwater and the first time the tip of the steeple emerged. I won't see it again. At least, I hope I won't."

"I have something of yours." I opened my change purse and took out the miraculous medal. "Your mother's name was Annette Manning."

"I thought you would find out eventually. Thank you, Chris. I've missed this. My mother died young, in her fifties, and this came to me. I'm glad it was you who found it."

"Henry Degenkamp saw you that night. I think he told Fred Larkin, but they kept it to themselves."

"It was a kind of round-robin blackmail of which I was reluctantly a part."

"Tell me if I have it right," I said. "J.J. Eberling made a deal with a general, who he probably knew through his father, to flood Studsburg instead of the neighboring farm area so that he would profit greatly and everyone else would profit some."

"J.J. owned more property in Studsburg than most people knew. He owned all the park area behind the church. He'd bought it up years ago, or his father had, when the local industry dried up. He had hopes of luring business to the town, but when he realized that was a dying dream, he lucked into this other way of getting rid of his unsalable property."

"And since Fred Larkin knew all about it, and also about J.J.'s indiscretions, he could twist J.J.'s arm if he had to, like the morning after the murder when he found the article about your time capsule."

"That was probably all the leverage he needed."

"Candy was Larkin's daughter from a casual affair in college in the thirties, and he never helped her mother or acknowledged his daughter."

"Both of which enraged her."

"So she threatened to expose his paternity if he didn't come clean on the payoff and get the town to pull out of it." The payoff had been the one thing Fred Larkin had never talked about.

"She was a girl who had worked hard for what she had, put herself through school with the help of a mother who nearly worked herself to death to keep them going. She hated greed, especially greed at the expense of other people, taxpayers like herself and her mother."

"I wonder," I said, "how she knew about the deal in the first place. She was an outsider."

"I told her."

"Yes, of course. And you were the reason her threat against Larkin failed."

"We were lovers," Father Hartman said, perhaps for the first time aloud. "And Fred Larkin found out."

I pulled my hasty sketch of Studsburg out of my bag and unfolded it. Joseph had said I needed it more than she did. For her, it had all been a question of geography. She had placed the medal on the sketch of St. Mary Immaculate, which was a brisk walk from the athletic field.

"She used to park her car at the athletic field during ball games and visit you in the rectory."

"That's right. How do you know all this?"

"Everybody saw her car there. It couldn't have been much of a walk to the church."

"It wasn't."

"Did Candy know about the time capsule?"

"It was her idea. She had a powerful interest in history. She wanted to be remembered." His voice broke and I looked away.

"I'm told it was Gwen Larkin who killed her," I said. "I'd guess Fred came to you and confessed everything he knew to keep you from talking. In return, he kept quiet about your relationship with Candy. Even when I saw him the last time, he never said a word. I think a lot of people in Studsburg may have known, or guessed. At first I thought it was Larkin they were all protecting. After a while I decided it was you. They guessed you'd made a clean break with Candy and they wanted you to go in peace."

"You're right about everything, Chris. We fell in love in the spring, an accident as these things always are. It was the happiest time of my life, and the only time I broke my vows or was tempted to. When school was over, Candy left. That was supposed to be it. I didn't even have her new address. Except that she wanted to be there that last morning to put the coins in the opening in the basement. But she never came. When I went down on the fifth, I couldn't understand why she would have sealed up the hole without putting the coins in. I thought she was trying to tell me something that I wasn't smart enough to figure out. I tried to get in touch with her, but I was never able to."

"And then you found out what happened when Fred Larkin came to you and confessed."

He was silent.

"It must have been a powerful urge that made you open that grave in the church last fall."

When he responded, his voice was strained. "I wanted to see for myself. I had agonized for thirty years over her death and her life, over the fact that she hadn't had a proper burial, the fact that I really caused her death."

"You didn't, Father."

"If we hadn't had our relationship, she might have been able to carry off her crusade against the Studsburg payoff. But Fred Larkin learned about our affair, and he told her he would make it public if she carried out her threat. She was protecting me by keeping quiet. Before I became part of it, there was a kind of balance of power between Larkin and Eberling. I knew all the rumors—I don't have to tell you how I knew; I'm sure you can guess—but I wasn't part of it. With our relationship, I was drawn into the circle. The balance now included me. Candy lost her leverage."

I opened my bag and took out the two letters I had found in Pennsylvania. "These are yours. I promise they've never been opened."

He pulled a handkerchief out of his pocket and held it to his eyes. "Thank you," he said. "It's so long ago and I behaved so badly and I loved her so much."

There was a sudden shout from a cluster of people near the edge of the basin. We looked toward the lake. The tip of the steeple was just disappearing as the water lapped over it. The TV crew was at work with its camera, and nearby I could see a young woman, her hair carefully sprayed in place, her coat a beautiful, photogenic shade of blue, standing with a microphone.

We walked to the edge, keeping out of the way of the crew

and the other onlookers. In a few seconds, I could no longer find the spot in the water where the steeple had been.

I turned to Father Hartman as he crossed himself.

Almost immediately the TV crew started to pack their equipment in the van, and the woman in the blue coat conferred with someone before walking away from the bank of the lake. For them the story was over and they would look ahead to the next one. The other onlookers also lost interest pretty quickly. We were alone, an ex-nun who had solved an unhappy puzzle and an aging priest whose rather handsome features were starting to show the effects of time, and perhaps of much more.

"I'd like to ask you a favor, Father," I said in the welcome silence. "I wonder if you would hear my confession."

He said, "I—" and stopped as though I had requested something he was unable to deliver. Then, summoning forty years of practice, he became a priest once more. "I'd be happy to, Chris. Where would you like to go?"

"I think right here would be just fine." I turned toward the lake and my memory of St. Mary Immaculate and repeated the words I had learned in my youth. "Bless me, Father, for I have sinned."

33

The killing in the church was a desecration. Only when the desecration became public knowledge, that is, known outside the confessional, did St. Mary Immaculate require resanctification. As far as I know, that has not been done. Perhaps the Catholic Church, in its wisdom, decided to wait for the next emergence of the town to resanctify the church. For an institution that has lasted as long as this one has, another thirty—or even a hundred—years is only a brief time. And by then all the principals are likely to be gone.

I went over the contents of Candy's two suitcases one last time, finding only one small item that I had overlooked before. I gave her clothing and the bags to Good Will and turned over all the papers except for one to Deputy Drago. The investigation into the murder of Candida Phillips had stalled, and no one was particularly anxious to keep it going now that the TV cameras weren't around. What he did with them was his business.

The last piece of paper, I burned in my fireplace. It was a receipt for a .38-caliber revolver bought by Candy Phillips before she came to Studsburg.

THE SAINT PATRICK'S DAY MURDER

by
Lee Harris

**The luck of the Irish
is about to run out.**

Coming soon to a bookstore near you.

Published by Fawcett Books.

THE GOOD FRIDAY MURDER

Christine Bennett has just left the cloistered world
of the nuns when she is enlisted to solve a forty-
year-old murder. Pursuing this mission with her old
religious zeal, she'll move heaven and earth to exon-
erate a pair of retarded savant twins, now senior
citizens, of their mother's murder on Good Friday
in 1950.

THE YOM KIPPUR MURDER

When ex-nun Chris Bennett can't get into Mr.
Herskovitz's apartment to accompany him to Yom
Kippur services, she discovers that her friend has
been murdered. The police arrest someone almost
immediately, but Chris is not convinced, and she is
determined to uncover the sacrilegious truth.

Look for the novels by

LEE HARRIS

in your local bookstore or...